WINTER UNDER THE COVERS

A ROSEDALE NOVEL

ELLE WATERS

This is a work of fiction. Names, places, organizations, and events are either products of the author's imagination or are used entirely fictitiously.

Copyright © 2025 by Elle Waters

All rights reserved.

ALSO BY ELLE WATERS

His Birthday Wish

His Christmas Love Song

His Fake Wedding Date

New Beginnings

Day Dreaming

His Ever After Collection

Rosedale

His Coffee Shop Crush

Rosedale Seasons

Cool for the Summer

Autumn Crush

Winter Under the Covers

A Small Town Spring

For Tom

ONE
CONNOR

"OKAY, we are thirty days from my wedding, so that means I'm delegating."

I blink sleepily at my sister and reach for the electric kettle, testing the temperature with a quick tap of my finger. Ouch. Hot. I pour water over my tea bag into an oversized monstrosity of a mug with a cartoon of an extremely alert-looking tabby and the word "catfeinated" stamped across it. I assume it was a gift from one of my mom's fans—her patients love her. And she loves them. I stifle my vague jealousy of Rosedale's pet population and respond to my sister.

"Do you have to delegate at six thirty in the morning?" I ask, breathing in the steam coming off my strong black tea.

Courtney, two years younger than me but twice as bossy, shoots me a look. "I have to be at work in half an hour, so yes. Mom's taking the brunt of things with the venue and the caterers, thank god. Dad's in charge of tracking down the RSVPs—we have to give final numbers soon. Mike's making sure the groomsmen are organized. God, I hope Binky doesn't ruin my wedding."

"Binky?"

"Mike's cousin. Don't worry. You'll meet him." Courtney puts a hand on her chest. "Oh my god. I'm freaking out."

I laugh because, despite her words, she looks perfectly calm. My family isn't big on emoting. I squeeze her shoulder reassuringly. "Hey, everything is going to be fine. You're the most organized person I know. You're going to have a beautiful wedding."

"Thanks. I know it's all going to be okay. It's just that I'm only going to do this once. I want it to be unforgettable."

"It will be. You picked a great guy, and it's going to be a great wedding."

She smiles and pushes her straight brown hair behind her ears to reveal small diamond studs that have nothing on the rock on her ring finger. My soon-to-be-brother-in-law, Mike, did not stint on the ring.

"Thanks, Connor. Speaking of numbers—are you bringing anyone to the wedding?"

I take a measured breath, take an experimental sip of my tea. Too hot. "No, I'll be flying solo."

"Are you sure you don't want to bring anyone? Not even a—friend? From Chicago?" She looks at me with her big brown eyes and I wonder if I'm reading too much into her words.

If there was someone I actually wanted to bring as my date to my little sister's wedding, this would be the perfect time to casually say, "Yeah, now that you mention it, I'll be bringing my hot boyfriend, who happens to be a Luke Evans look-alike. And by the way, if you hadn't guessed sometime in the past twenty-eight years, I'm gay."

But since I don't have anything close to a boyfriend, there's no reason to out myself at the crack of dawn on a Wednesday morning. Not when my sister has enough stress about this wedding as it is.

So I shrug, slipping into the version of myself I stick to when I'm at home in Rosedale. "Nope. Feel free to give my plus-one to someone else," I add, pretending we're having a conversation about numbers, not my love life.

"Okay." It's stupid to feel disappointed that she doesn't probe further. "Hey, isn't it your first day in the office?"

"Yep." It's the only reason I'm awake at this ungodly hour. It's not even light outside. The veterinary office opens at eight on weekdays and I had overly optimistic ideas about getting in a session on the treadmill in my parents' basement before leaving for work. "So, it seems like you have everything wedding-related covered."

"Actually, I need you to do one thing for me. Two things," she adds quickly.

"I already have my suit and tie in the specified color scheme. What else is there?" Mike asked me to be one of his six groomsmen, and since Courtney is my only sibling, I was happy to be included, even if Mike and I aren't particularly close. I've only met the guy a few times on the rare occasions I've been back to Rosedale since I started veterinary school.

"One, I need you to watch out for Mike at the bachelor party. Don't let his frat boy friends let him do something stupid."

"Like what?"

"Like whatever," she says, her voice ending on a whine. "I don't want any trips to the emergency room. Or jail. He's a high school teacher, for goodness' sake."

"I'll do my best," I agree solemnly, taking a sip of my still-scalding tea.

"Okay, then there's the flowers."

"For the bachelor party?" I really need more sleep for this conversation, but I was tossing and turning in the guest bed in my old room, unsuccessfully trying not to stress over starting work today.

"No, for the wedding. I've been working with the guy at the flower shop next to the office. Since you'll be right there, I was thinking you could stop in and make sure everything is okay with our order. I haven't had a chance to go myself. Please?"

She never asks me for anything, so I instantly give in.

"I don't know anything about flowers," I warn her.

"Neither do I, but the guy who works there does. He's a pro. I just need you to confirm the order. He has Dad's credit card on file."

"Today?"

"Today, tomorrow. Whenever you have time. Thanks, Connor. I gotta go." She gives me a tight smile and gathers her bag. "I'll see you later."

"Hey—are you okay? Besides the wedding stuff?" I know she's under a lot of stress with the wedding, but she's usually completely in control, executing the life plan she made when she was twelve. Graduate high school at the top of her class, finish college in five years with her teaching credential and a master's degree, get a job and work on her PhD in administration so she could one day become a principal. Along the way, she met Mike, who's a teacher, too, and a volleyball coach. When she called last year to tell me Mike proposed, I'd never heard her sound so happy.

"What? I'm fine." I'm not surprised by her terse answer, but then she does something shocking and pulls me into a hug—we're not a hugging sort of family. "Connor, I'm really glad you're home for a while. And not only because we need your help right now."

My dad, still in his pajamas, wanders into the kitchen with our geriatric white Labrador mix Snowy—Courtney named him after the dog from the *Tin Tin* comics—at his heels.

"Hi, Dad, bye, Dad," Courtney says. "I'm off to school."

Dad waves at her absently. "Have a good day."

I open a few cupboard doors at random, not finding what I need.

"What are you looking for?" Dad asks.

"Frying pan?"

He yawns, goes to a corner cupboard, pulls out a pan, and hands it to me while Snowy settles into his bed in the kitchen. "Your mother reorganized yesterday. Her version of taking it easy." He runs a hand over his short, graying beard. He's built like me, five-eight, strong thighs and shoulders, and a full head of chocolate brown hair a shade darker than our eyes, though his is more gray than brown at this point. "It's good you were able to come help, or she'd be trying to see patients today."

I wasn't exactly angling for a job in my mom's veterinary office, but she slipped on some ice and broke her arm badly a few days ago. When my Aunt Violet, who runs the front office, called and asked if I would fill in for a while, I immediately said yes. I think my aunt was surprised by how quickly I agreed; I was surprised, too.

Rosedale wasn't on my short list of places to go after getting my Doctor of Veterinary Medicine. For so many reasons. But I could read between the lines of my aunt's request. If Mom couldn't find anyone suitable to replace her, she'd go back to the office too soon and risk injuring herself further.

Since I graduated, I've been filling in at a large animal hospital, which meant a flexible schedule and no contract to break. Why shouldn't I use my flexibility to help my family? And even if this is just a temporary stop on my path to figuring out my long-term career, the timing works well with Courtney's wedding coming up in a few short weeks.

As I chow down on my eggs, I realize I have to skip the treadmill and hustle to be at work on time. Which in Dr. Nieves's eyes means being early.

Speak of the devil—my mom, already fully dressed, appears just as I'm putting my dishes in the dishwasher.

"Morning, Mom."

"Connor." Iris Nieves glances at the oven clock and then at me, lifting a single pale eyebrow. Her fine blonde hair and blue eyes didn't make their way to either Courtney or me. "You better get going."

My stomach jumps with the implication that I'm already failing at filling in for her. I might have followed in her footsteps, but she's always had an air of skepticism about my wanting to be a vet. I think she expected me to flame out somewhere along the way.

But now I'll have a firsthand opportunity to show her the kind of vet I am.

"Almost ready," I say. "Can I get the keys?"

She purses her lips, disappears into her office, a small room off the kitchen that at one time was a pantry, and comes back with a key ring with keys to the office and her SUV. She'd reluctantly agreed to let me borrow her car after the doctor forbade her from driving. "Ridiculous man," she'd scoffed, as if forbidding a person with an arm recently broken in two places to drive was an outrageous imposition.

"Call me if you have any issues."

"You're not going to come in later?" When I arrived yesterday, we'd gone over the week's schedule, and she'd given me a long list of reminders. The way she's done things for twenty-five years isn't all that different from my own approach, most of which I learned by watching her. But she'd also mentioned that she'd be coming into the office to do paperwork, the subtext being she'd be there to check up on me.

"No, she's not," my dad answers for her. "The doctor said absolutely no work for the first week. She's going to be in the den watching *Sex and the City* reruns."

I burst out with a little laugh. I try to picture my mom being captivated by the antics of Carrie and friends and fail.

Mom shows a hint of a smile. "I was thinking more like working on my wedding speech."

"As long as you're using dictation and not typing," Dad decrees. "Now, Connor will call you if he needs to, and you will let your son get to work."

I take the exit and run upstairs to throw on my work scrubs and tennis shoes. Being a vet is a physical job—there's a lot of lifting, standing, and getting down on the floor with skittish patients. Even if my stomach's jumpy with nerves at the prospect of messing this up, I am actually looking forward to getting back into a work routine. The days are never dull when you're working with animals.

I grab a bottled smoothie drink out of the fridge, holler goodbye to my parents, and take Mom's SUV out of the garage to drive the eight minutes from our turn-of-the-last-century colonial-style house on the outskirts of Rosedale to downtown. Nieves Veterinary Care is on Linden, just off Main. It's at the end of a short block across from a furniture store that takes up the entire other side of the street. NVC is in the largest of four units on the ground floor of a two-story building with a stone facade that also houses an insurance office, a currently empty storefront, and the flower shop Courtney mentioned.

I used to love visiting my mom here. When I was little, I liked seeing the variety of animals in the waiting room. Later, I was fascinated by the instruments and X-ray machine, the soothing way my mom spoke to her patients and their owners. She was always so calm, so reassuring. She used a tone of voice with them that I rarely heard at home. I think I felt closest to her here. It's certainly where she always seemed happiest.

And maybe choosing to follow in her footsteps and become a vet was my way of trying to show her that even if she wasn't as empathetic with me as she was with other people's animals, I loved her anyway.

I park behind the building. There's a single row of parking spaces, a few allotted to each of the businesses. My aunt's Corolla is already there in one of the NVC spots. I use Mom's key to let myself in the back door. The security system has been deactivated and the lights are already on, the heat a welcome reprieve from the chilly January morning. I stash my smoothie in the break room's fridge, pass the storage room, the three exam rooms, and the imaging room, and find my aunt in the front office-slash-waiting room. This is Violet's domain. She rules as a benign dictator, keeping waiting patients separate and calm with her stash of dog and cat treats and lollipops for concerned children.

"Hey, Aunt Violet."

"Connor, you're here," she notes briskly. "We've got back-to-back appointments today since we had to shift everyone who was scheduled earlier this week. The vet tech is running late, of course. It's going to be a busy day. I hope you're up for it."

I've been working at one of the largest veterinary practices in Cook County for the past six months. I don't have enough experience yet to say I've seen it all, but I'm pretty confident that I can handle whatever the dogs and cats of Rosedale can throw at me.

"Don't worry. I got this."

She pats me on the shoulder. "Of course you do. And you look so handsome in your scrubs. We should take some pictures of you for our social media profiles. I bet we get some new clients who want to see the hot new vet."

"Auntie! That's so inappropriate." I feel my cheeks heating. "And since when does Mom do social media?"

"She doesn't—I do. We've got to keep up with the times, after all."

"My bad." I make a mental note to follow the office from my personal account later. "It's almost time to open. You ready?"

"I'm ready," Violet announces. "Let's do this."

TWO
SHAY

I'M lucky I have the shortest commute in Rosedale.

I forgot to set my alarm, and when I peek out from under my quilt to sleepily grab my phone, it's after nine. I swear, and sit up, knocking my head on the slanted ceiling that's been the bane of my existence since I moved into the second-floor apartment over the flower shop.

I rub the perpetual tender spot on my head and get out of bed, careful not to stand all the way up until I get to the middle of the room where the ceiling's apex gives me a few inches above my six-one frame. The tiny bedroom is squeezed under the eve of the roof, with a legal-pad-sized window looking onto Linden Street below. It's a great place to fall asleep on rainy nights— built-in ASMR—but a terrible place to get dressed when you're still half asleep.

I bring my clothes with me to the bathroom, thankful for the normal eight-foot ceiling in here, and grateful that the apartment has reliable heat. We've been having a cold January, and even though this is my second New

England winter, my blood hasn't yet thickened up to true local levels.

On goes a thermal long-sleeved tee and warm corduroys that I actually like, even though I'd never owned a pair before moving to Connecticut. I pull on my wool socks, my lined boots, and a denim button-down. I'll bring a sweater down to the shop, but honestly, once I start moving around, I'll be plenty warm. I keep the shop comfortable for the tropical houseplants we carry, plus the plants give off heat of their own. They breathe like humans, and when they exhale, moisture enters the air, just like us.

On the efficiency-sized stove in the open kitchen, I make myself a quick fried egg sandwich—I won't last long without protein—and scarf it down while checking on the seedings and succulents I have incubating under grow lights in the living room side of the apartment. Everything looks happy, which makes me happy.

I trail my fingers over one smooth aloe leaf, then duck back into the bathroom to brush my teeth and use my electric razor to smooth away the fine blond hairs on my cheeks and chin. I take a precious minute to brush out my naturally bleach-blond shoulder-length hair and make sure I have an elastic—or three—in the jangle of bracelets around my wrist. My hair elastics tend to go missing and I hate not having one to pull my hair back with when I need it, but for now I leave my hair loose. Once I grab my phone, I'm ready for the day.

Now for my commute. It takes me all of thirty seconds to trot down the back stairs and unlock the back entrance to Rosedale Flowers and More. I'm immediately hit by a wave of the best smell on earth—the scent of living plants. The shop's air is clean and earthy, with a hint of sweetness from the cut flowers we also carry.

Rosedale Flowers and More was your typical small-town flower shop when I started working here. Its bread and butter was assembling and delivering get well baskets, funeral arrangements, and my personal favorite, bridal bouquets, plus corsages during prom season and red roses on Valentine's Day. But over the past year I've introduced live houseplants, bulbs, seeds, gardening tools, and gift items in my quest to turn the flower shop into a plant shop. I've really been focusing on the "and More" in the name.

The owner, Rodney Greer, basically doesn't care what I do with the shop as long as it at least breaks even. He owns the entire building in addition to the flower shop itself. The partial second story, only half as deep as the ground floor, is divided up equally between the four units and serves as extra storage space for his tenants, except for my apartment. Rodney told me he'd once planned to turn all of the second-floor spaces into apartments, but after seeing the results of the first one, decided against it. After eighteen months of banging my head on the slanted ceilings, I think he made the right call.

But sore head aside, I love it here.

Rosedale is the quintessential New England small town I grew up idolizing in movies and TV shows, with its brick-lined downtown, charming wood frame houses, maple trees with fat green leaves in spring that turn crispy red in fall, and the promise of snow all winter long.

As a kid in Scottsdale, Arizona, seasons were this

magical thing that happened in other places. I'd always planned to make a big dramatic move once I grew up. But one thing after another kept me in the Grand Canyon state—my parents said they'd pay for college, but only if I went locally. Then I got a great job at a big nursery that meant I could turn down my dad's offer to buy me my own franchise. He owns fourteen Burger Busters in ten cities and would love nothing more than for me to follow in his footsteps the way my older brother Tye has—Tye's got two locations and counting.

Eventually I burned out on the nursery job, and then my on-again-off-again relationship ended for good. When the algorithm fed me a video about the best small towns in Connecticut, I took a shot and cold called the one business in town I was qualified to work at.

Rodney, who'd been running the place single-handedly since his wife died, grabbed the chance to step back from the business and hired me over the phone. I was an official Rosedale resident three weeks later. He trained me for about a week and then set me loose. I embraced the freedom to do my own thing, while establishing my brand new, four-seasons life.

I get paid in board—I don't pay rent to live in the apartment—and in commissions on the events I book. It's the arrangement we made a year and a half ago when I was desperate to start fresh. The working situation is admittedly unusual, but it's been fun to put my own stamp on this place, to see if I could modernize it. Being the only employee except for a couple of retired ladies who pitch in when there's a big event like a wedding is challenging—I had to close the shop entirely for a couple of days last month when I had a cold. But I've managed.

Now that I've gotten the hang of retail in a small town, I've been imagining what it would be like to own a shop of my own. Retail is in my blood, after all, but I've never wanted a cookie cutter business like my parents and brother. As much fun as running Rosedale Flowers and More is, I'd love to own my own place, to profit from its success and feel like I'm building my own legacy. Of course, I'd need money to do that, but I'm working on it. I've always been a good saver, and even if my income has been unpredictable since I took this job, my expenses are low.

I push all of that to the back of my brain while I run through my opening routine. First, I turn on the lights, then put on the music, usually classic rock or eighties pop. Then I wake up the tablet computer we use as the point of sale and count out the cash drawer, making a mental note that I should get more singles from the bank. I unlock the front door and turn the carved wooden sign from closed to open. In the summer, I leave the door invitingly ajar, but it's barely above freezing today, so the door remains shut.

On a winter weekday we'll get a few walk-ins and phone orders, but usually I'm focused on tending to what's in stock, watering and pruning, making reorders, and preparing for any upcoming events. This weekend I'm doing a flower arrangement for an anniversary party and the favors for a baby shower. Those will be fun—I've potted up baby succulents in miniature terracotta pots that I'll decorate with some green and yellow ribbon. The parents specified the colors for their gender-neutral shower.

The computer makes inventory a breeze, but I prefer to do my planning for events on paper. I'm hunched over the counter, looking at my notes for the baby shower, when my cell rings. I don't have to look at the screen to know it's my mom. She calls me every Wednesday, and if I don't pick up, she'll just call every few hours until I do.

I decide to get this week's call over with. "Hey, Mom."

"Hey, Blueberry," she says with her bright voice, using the nickname I acquired as a blue-eyed baby. "I checked the weather for Rosedale and it's chilly over there. Are you dressed warm enough?"

"I am, actually. I'm twenty-nine. I know how to dress for the cold," I say mildly.

"I know how old you are." She laughs as if I've made a hilarious joke. "Daddy and I were just talking about how you're going to be thirty this year. We won't mention how old that makes me. Do you want to do something big for it? We could have a party at the country club. Or we could do a family trip. How does Mexico sound?"

My birthday isn't until September. "Uh. I'll think about it."

"If we want a good date at the club, we'd have to book soon. How are things?"

"Pretty much the same as the last time we talked. Working. How are things going at—" I have to stop myself from saying home. "—the house?"

"Oh, we still have all the Christmas stuff up. I'll get the girls to take everything down in a couple of days."

I wince. "The girls" are what my mom calls the women who come in to clean her and my father's 9,000 square foot McMansion.

"And your daddy's thinking about opening another Burger Buster in Tucson. We're always busy, Blueberry, but we miss you."

"I know. I miss you, too." It's not a lie. I used work as an excuse not to come home for the holidays, and it was the first Christmas I'd spent on my own. At the time, I'd wanted to avoid the endless hints, subtle and not-so-subtle, that I should move back to Scottsdale. My parents haven't been reticent about telling me how they feel about my living in a different time zone. They thought I was joking when I told them I had plans to move to a town in Connecticut they'd never heard of.

When they bought me a plane ticket to come home that first Christmas, I couldn't say no. For one thing, I was lonely. I'd only been in Rosedale for a few months, and I'd started to make friends, but didn't have a good reason not to head back to Arizona for a few days. But this year I actually had friends who invited me to share in some of their festivities. I went to Jack and Pete's for a cozy Christmas Eve party, and joined Meadow and Melissa at Sparkle, the gay bar in Midville, on New Year's Eve, where I ended up making out with a very cute out-of-towner who looked a bit like Pedro Pascal, at least with champagne goggles on. It wasn't a bad way to ring in the new year.

"Maybe Daddy and I should come visit you," she says. "We could go skiing."

This is new. "Um, Rosedale isn't exactly near any ski

spots," I say, "but you're welcome to come visit. Just not around Valentine's Day—I'll be slammed with work." I already have more pre-orders for bouquets than I can comfortably handle alone.

"Okay, Blueberry, I'll look at the calendar. You sure you don't want me to ask Carrie at the nursery if you can have your old job back?"

"No, Mom. I have a job. In fact, it's really busy at the shop, so I'm going to have to go." I look around the empty store. "Talk to you later."

"Love you."

"Love you, too." I hang up with a sense of relief. I love my family, but my mom has smothering tendencies. As much as we love each other, I've had to put a heavy foot down to try for true independence.

Maybe it would be good for Mom and Dad to visit, so they can see how normal Rosedale is, how far the shop has come along. Maybe then they'd stop bugging me about coming back to Arizona.

Hey, a guy can dream.

THREE
SHAY

I SLIP out of the flower shop in the early afternoon, leaving my usual "back in fifteen minutes" sign on the door, and go to Hot Brew for the caffeine fix I missed in this morning's rush.

There's a pretty big lunch crowd, but I'm not stressed about getting back to the shop. One of the nice things about Rosedale is that people don't expect you to be available 24/7. If someone comes by and I'm not there, they'll just come back later.

I wait my turn in line, using my phone to post about the new seed starting kits in the shop. Even though we're still in the middle of winter, spring isn't too far off.

Ruth's at the register, and Meadow's making drinks. "Hey girls, how's business?"

Ruth just gives me a smile—not known for her conversational skills, that one. But Meadow answers, "Busy. I think everyone's already given up on their New Year's resolutions."

"That's why I never make any," I say.

"I thought you said it's because you're perfect the way you are," Meadow replies tartly.

"That too, obviously." I ask Ruth for a flat white and a turkey avocado sandwich, my go-to lunch on the days I don't have the foresight to make food to bring to the shop. Which is honestly most days.

I scroll through my feed while I wait, then stick my phone in the back pocket of my corduroys so I have both hands free to take the flat white Meadow carries out to me. She knows I hate those plastic to-go lids and hasn't given me one, but it makes the drink precarious.

"So did you ever text the guy from New Year's Eve?" she asks as I warm my hands on the cup and blow across the surface.

I wrinkle my nose. "No. I didn't even bother to save his number."

"Why not? He was cute," she says.

"He lives in the city. I'm not doing long distance."

"It's a pain, but what are your other options? You can't wait until Jack and Pete turn this place into a certified gay colony of all their friends."

"That doesn't sound too terrible. Their friends are all pretty cute." As a guest at their wedding this past summer, I can attest to that.

"All I'm saying is I bet that guy would make a point of coming up this way for you."

"That's sweet." I think it over. The guy had been the perfect New Year's Eve stress release, but I'm honestly happier spending time with my friends and work than chasing after boys. Rosedale may be gay-friendly, but it's still a small town. The pickings are slim, and trying to find an actual boyfriend seems like an exhausting prospect. "I'm not really looking for anything right now." True enough.

Meadow smiles slyly. "But you aren't not looking."

"I'm not not looking," I confirm, because hell, if Jonathan Bailey walked through my door and swept me off my feet, I wouldn't cry about it.

Ruth arrives with my sandwich wrapped in brown paper. "I gotta jet back to work." I drop a kiss on Meadow's cheek and head back to the flower shop, glad for my warm coat and scarf against the chilly air.

The afternoon goes by quickly, and I'm putting together a re-order for cute vintage-inspired watering cans we sold a lot of during the holiday season when the door opens and a guy comes in, looking around the store curiously before his gaze lands on me.

"Hello," he says, and the single word sends a zing of awareness through me. Uh-oh. He's cute—really cute, a thick head of dark brown hair, thick black eyebrows to match, a jawline that reminds me of a member of a boy band I had a crush on once upon a time. He's wearing a navy blue peacoat over dark green scrubs, his hands hidden in the pockets. I've never seen him before, and I find myself absolutely compelled to learn what he needs from me.

Probably an anniversary bouquet for his girlfriend. Ah well, such is life.

He strolls up to the counter, looking more at me than at the shop.

"What can I do for you?" I say, with a hint of flirtation, because why not? It's my shop. Basically.

"Hello," he says again. He kind of shakes himself and elaborates. "I'm Courtney Nieves's brother. She asked me to stop by and make sure you had everything you need for her wedding order." His voice is a tenor, not exactly high-pitched, but on the softer side. And he's not here for a girlfriend. He's not Jonathan Bailey, but I'm not not looking.

I set aside my watering can order and turn my full attention to him. "Nice to meet you, Courtney Nieves's brother. Let me grab my notes. It's the Valentine's Day wedding, right?"

"Yep. And it's Connor, by the way. Might be more efficient than saying Courtney Nieves's brother all the time." His smile is a little shy and very attractive.

I let my own smile grow larger than I usually offer this early in an interaction with a customer. "I'm Shay Brierley."

"Nice to meet you, Shay," he says, holding my gaze for a beat with his big brown eyes.

I rummage under the counter for a second and come up with my large, well-used Moleskine. I flip a few pages and find my notes on the wedding order in question. "Courtney and Mike," I read off the paper. "'Winter Romance' theme. Red and white roses, baby's breath, very classic. Centerpieces for the tables, number to be determined, two large arrangements for the reception, hair pieces for six bridesmaids and the MOB, boutonnieres for six groomsmen plus one for the groom, and a medium bouquet for the bride." I look across the counter at Connor. "Is that what you have?"

He rubs the back of his neck and smiles sheepishly. "What's MOB?"

"Mother of the bride."

"Oh, that makes sense. It sounds great to me. I'm one of the groomsmen, so, yeah. Sounds like you have every-thing under control."

"All I need is the final number of centerpieces. And your sister paid a deposit when she placed the initial order. Should I just charge the card on file for the balance?"

"Go ahead. When do you need to know about the centerpieces?"

"Oh, a week or two before should be okay." I make a note to remind myself to follow up about that if I don't hear from Courtney, or her cute brother, before then. "So, are you in healthcare?" If he tells me he's a nurse, I'm definitely hitting on him.

He looks down at his scrubs, then back up at me. "I'm a vet."

Good enough. Animal lover. Smart. And his lack of hat and scarf makes more sense now. "You work next door?"

"Yeah, just started. It's my mom's practice, but she broke her arm, and with the wedding coming up, I'm filling in."

"Ah." So he's not exactly local. "You're new to town?"

"I arrived yesterday, actually. But I grew up here in Rosedale."

"Nice place to grow up."

His laugh is a little bitter. "It was more boring than you can imagine. I got out as soon as I could."

"Boring is relative." I get wanting to escape your hometown, but I feel defensive on my adopted town's behalf.

"How long have you been here?" he asks, looking around the shop again. "When I was a kid, this place was very different."

"Let's see." I pull an elastic band from my wrist and gather my hair in one hand, twisting it into a messy bun and holding it in place with a snap. I watch him watch me do it and gain confidence. My hair is my barometer for attraction. Straight boys ignore it, while the ones who find it as fascinating as this guy seems to usually don't mind some mild flirting. "I moved here the fall before last. So almost a year and a half now."

His brow knits together. "Why would you move to Rosedale, of all places?"

"I blame social media."

"Explain."

"Well, there I was, living in Scottsdale, Arizona, land of my birth, working at a huge nursery where I was just a cog in a machine, and scrolling the 'Gram on my lunch break when I came across a video about this quaint small town in Connecticut called Rosedale. I got a weird feeling I couldn't ignore. You ever get that?" I lean over the counter. "A gut feeling that you just know something's going to be important?"

Connor's Adam's apple bobs as he swallows hard and looks at the tattoos covering my left forearm. He moves his attention from my tats to my face and I swear I can feel his gaze like a touch on my skin. He doesn't say anything, just nods.

"Anyway, I always wanted to live someplace with seasons. I pitched myself to Rodney, the owner of this place, found myself with a job and even a place to live. The shop needed a lot of sprucing up, but I like hard work."

"But Rosedale? It's so—blah."

"What are you talking about? It's adorable. And there's actually a lot happening in town. The Art Center always has something going on. We've got a great farmers' market in the warmer months, some new shops. The best coffee in Connecticut is right here at Hot Brew, just around the corner."

"I don't drink coffee."

I straighten up, narrow my eyes at him. "Wow. You're a tough nut to crack. Where are you visiting us from, then?"

"I went to college and vet school in Chicago. I've been there for a few years," he says. "Not sure it's where I'll end up ultimately, but it's a great city."

Chicago, the perfect litmus test. "I went to Boystown for Pride a few years ago with my college BFF," I say casually. "We have some great stories."

He freezes. Boystown is Chicago's famous gay neighborhood. Here's his chance to pick up what I'm throwing down. I look at him, trying hard not to expect anything, and then he finally says, "They call it Northalsted now."

He *is* a tough nut to crack. I don't know how to take that, but I'm not ready to admit defeat yet. I wrinkle my nose. "That's...way not as sexy."

He shrugs. "Yeah, well, I think it was a business decision."

As a businessman, I get it. You don't want to scare off the straight dollars. "Okay, I guess I can see it. Well, Rosedale isn't exactly Boystown, but we are getting something of a reputation for being a mini-inland-Provincetown."

"Seriously?" He looks as if I just claimed they were moving the White House and making Rosedale the nation's new capital. "How so?"

"Honestly, I don't know how much is just hype from one of our more famous residents, Jack Avery. He's an author, and he's always talking up the town. His cousin moved here last year, opened a cookie shop."

"I have heard of the cookie shop. My sister's getting custom sugar cookies as wedding favors for all of her guests, and she was raving about the place."

One last try, then. "So, are you a chocolate person or a fruit person?"

He blinks. For a guy who went to I don't know how many years of school to become a vet, he's slow on the uptake. "Excuse me?"

"Because Beck makes these chocolate chocolate chip cookies that are guaranteed to get your pulse racing, but if you're a fruit person, he also makes these apricot jelly things that will change your life. So, are you a chocolate person or a fruit person?"

He softens, lips curving upward. "Sounds like you're both."

"Gun to my head, I'd pick chocolate every time," I admit. "But variety is good."

"Is it cheating to say I'm actually more of a nut person?"

I smile widely at that. "No, nuts are the secret third option that proves you're not a lost cause because even better than the chocolate chocolate chip cookies are the pecan bars Beck made at Thanksgiving. I thought I was going to have to hold a demonstration to get him to keep them on the menu, but luckily there was enough demand that he makes them about once a week."

He looks intrigued. "Okay, I'm sold. Pecan bars sound amazing."

"It's Wednesday, right?" I look at him, and he nods. I think quickly about how best to play this. "Friday's usually when he does the pecan bars, but you have to go early before they sell out."

"Good to know." He hesitates, then adds, "I work early hours, so I'll probably miss my window."

Finally, he's giving me a proper opening. Inside I'm buzzing, but I know to play it cool.

"Hmmm." I close my notebook, openly look him up and down, from his sensible sneakers to his tousled hair that looks soft under the hint of gel. "I could be persuaded to pick up a pecan bar for you if you want to drop by later on Friday."

My pulse kicks up as if I've already eaten something sugary as I wait for his response.

He thinks for a moment—the longest moment of my life—then leans across the counter, coming within a foot of me. I smell antiseptic soap and something earthier underneath.

"How could I persuade you to do that?" he asks, the hint of a smile back on his face.

I'm quiet for a beat as I process that he's finally

flirting back. But then I shrug as if I couldn't care less. "You could buy something."

He looks around the shop, and I look too, trying to see it from his perspective. There's the display rack of greeting cards, some really beautiful handmade pottery, and lots and lots of plants. I wonder if he knows anything about plants, but then he walks over to the cards, thumbing through the assortment. He chuckles at a couple of the more amusing ones, then grabs one with a simple line drawing of a leafy green potted plant with the word "thanks" letter-pressed on the front. He brings it to me, not making eye contact as he produces his wallet from the inside pocket of his coat.

"Just the card?" I ask, my voice suddenly throaty.

"For now, yeah." He hands over his credit card and declines a receipt. But after the transaction is over, he points to the pen resting next to my notebook. "May I?"

Mystified, I hand it over. He accepts it with strong-looking, blunt fingers with neatly trimmed nails.

He opens the card, thinks for a second, then scribbles a note. He returns the pen, puts the card in its oatmeal-gray envelope. He doesn't seal it, just offers it to me. I take it, a touch bewildered. I glance at him in question. I wasn't expecting this. His smile is nervous now, which makes me melt, but he says, "Open it."

I slide the card out and read the message inside. I give a short, pleased laugh, then read the words out loud. "Dear Shay, thanks in advance for the pecan bar. I'm sure it was delicious. Connor." He even spelled my name right.

"You have to get me one now," he says. "Otherwise it'll mess with the space-time continuum or something."

"We wouldn't want that." I'm delighted at the impetuous gesture, and the promise that I'm going to get to see him again.

"I better let you get back to work."

"Okay." I tuck the card inside my notebook, already knowing I'm going to read it about a dozen times before Friday.

The smile Connor gives me as he backs away from the counter is sweetly genuine.

I can't help wanting to confirm already. "See you Friday?"

"See you Friday, Shay."

He walks out and turns left out the door in the direction of the veterinarian's office. I suddenly have a pecan bar date with a cute vet.

FOUR
CONNOR

I WAKE up early enough on my second full day in Rosedale to get a few minutes in on the treadmill, then shower before work. I even have time to realize there's not a whole lot of food in the fridge for either breakfast or lunch. Even though I'm staying with my parents, it's not their job to feed me. I'll have to get some groceries on the way home from work. Shay mentioned the coffee shop in town—surely they can offer me something for breakfast?

Besides, maybe it's time I educate myself about this apparently new and improved Rosedale. Shay's promise that the town has more to offer than I remember feels far-fetched, but I'm willing to give the guy the benefit of the doubt.

It's been hard to think about much else besides Shay since meeting him yesterday. The last thing I expected on this trip home was to meet someone, but I was instantly attracted to the flower shop proprietor, initially snared by his distractingly long white-blond hair, narrow straight nose, and saucy smile, then reeled in by his forearm of tattoos and the way I couldn't quite figure out if his light eyes were blue or green in the mellow store lighting.

His gentle-yet-unambiguous flirting was refreshing and impossible to resist. Maybe it's pointless to get involved with someone when I'm only supposed to be here until Mom's arm heals up, but I remind myself that all I've agreed to is sharing a pecan bar with the guy, not getting matching tattoos.

I wonder if he's got tats anywhere else on his long, lean body?

I drag my mind back to the task at hand—feeding myself. I drive to Main Street, and it takes me a minute to find parking, which surprises me at seven in the morning. I finally get a street spot a couple of blocks past my destination.

I wrap my scarf around my neck to keep out the cold early morning wind and march toward the coffee shop, already anticipating the tea I'm going to order.

Hot Brew is all gleaming black and white tile and filled with the soothing buzz of conversation from patrons at cafe tables scattered around the space. It smells like coffee and cardamom, and my mouth instantly waters at the prospect of one of the flaky pastries in the case. This place reminds me of one of the local coffee shops in my old neighborhood, and yes, I guess I'm surprised that Rosedale has such a slick-but-cozy spot.

"How long have you been here?" is the first thing out of my mouth when I reach the counter and the pretty woman with exaggerated black eyebrows and matching lipstick who's waiting to take my order. She has a small silver ring through one of her eyebrows and an unim-pressed expression on her face.

"Connor Nieves," the woman says flatly. "Buy me a coffee first, would you?"

I peer at her more closely. "Oh my god, Meadow. Hi." We were in the same class in high school. What's more, we went to senior prom together, due to the fact neither of us had dates and I knew my parents would make a fuss if I tried to go solo. Meadow didn't have this gothic vibe back then—at least, not this overtly. She was a big reader, I remember. We were both quote-unquote smart kids and had a lot of the same classes. Prom with her was fun, if slightly awkward. We went as friends and ended up having a surprisingly good time dancing and making fun of the drunk couples and their drama.

"Heard you were in town," she says, sizing me up. "You're an animal doctor now?"

"Yep, an actual full-fledged veterinarian as of six months ago."

"Congratulations," she says, not a trace of enthusiasm in her voice. "And to answer your question, Hot Brew opened, oh, five years ago? I've been here since the begin-ning. Coffee is my calling."

It seems I've been missing out. "That's cool," I say. "Can I get a breakfast sandwich to go? And one of those sticky buns. And a large English Breakfast."

"You got it." She rings me up. "You know, I'm surprised you moved back here," she says, startling me with her candor. "You were so anxious to get out."

"Well, I haven't exactly moved back," I rush to say. "I'm just helping out for a while. My mom broke her arm, and my sister's getting married in a few weeks. There's a lot going on."

"Well, it's nice to see you, Connor," she says, sounding like she actually means it. She hands me a to-go cup with my tea.

"Thanks, you too."

While I wait for my food, I glance at the patrons. There's a mix of ages, some people alone with their coffee and their phones, a man with a little kid, and a couple of people working on laptops. It's not Chicago, but it's not bad. Not bad at all.

A twenty-something woman with wavy brown hair comes in and walks over to the opening behind the counter. "Babe, save my life," she says, and Meadow hands her a to-go cup like mine.

The girl kisses her on the mouth. "Thank you so much. Inventory is killing me."

"You think you'll be home for dinner?" Meadow asks.

"God, I hope so," the other woman says. "Is Fred going to be done with the sink, do you think?"

"It might be takeout again if not."

"Great. Okay, see you. Love you."

"Love you," Meadow returns easily, and the brown-haired girl leaves as quickly as she came.

I'm processing this interaction when a red-haired employee hands me a paper bag with my order. "Need anything else?" she asks softly.

"No, uh, thanks." I catch Meadow's eye as I get ready to leave and give her a shell-shocked wave.

She's got a girlfriend. Who she kisses at work. Suddenly, it makes so much sense why neither of us had dates to prom. After high school, I ran halfway across the country where I didn't know a soul in order to be myself. Meadow stayed behind, and she's got a girlfriend who she kisses at work in front of half the town. She's out, like Shay obviously is.

Jealousy keeps me company on the two-minute drive to work. Violet's beaten me in again. She goes over today's schedule with me while I eat my tasty breakfast sandwich.

"You ever go to Hot Brew?" I ask as we finish up.

"Now and then."

"It's nice. I don't remember anyone mentioning it when it opened up."

"Oh, like you've been so up on all the new businesses in Rosedale?" She gazes at me with skeptical eyes.

"Fair enough." I wipe my mouth, toss the wrapper I practically licked clean in the trash. "Did you know Meadow Beddingfield worked there?"

"She's worked there for years. She pretends to be mean, but she's a sweetie. We both volunteer at the biannual library book sale."

"Really? She seems to have changed a lot since we went to prom together."

"Hmm. She's got a girlfriend now, if that's what you mean. You're out of luck there, nephew."

I shift. I'm so used to being not-out when I come back home that it's a kind of persona I slip on. I've justified it to myself a million times. I'm not lying because I've never pretended to be straight—I'm not out there talking about made-up girlfriends or anything. But even back in

Chicago, I was guarded. I don't make a habit of blithely outing myself to everyone I meet.

And over the years, it feels harder and harder to say the truth to the people who have known me the longest.

"I saw her with her girlfriend," I say instead. "It's cool that they feel comfortable being out."

My aunt laughs at that. "You have been living under a rock. Rosedale's gotten positively progressive, dear. Should make you feel more at home."

I glance at her sharply. "What do you mean?"

"After your stint in the big city and all."

"Oh, right." I shake my head, annoyed at myself for my defensiveness. My meal weighs heavy in my stomach. I check my watch, then push up from the break table and go to wash my hands. "Time to open up."

NINE HOURS LATER, I roll my shoulders to get the kinks out. I say goodbye to Tara, the vet tech, and Aunt Violet, then climb into Mom's car. I punch in the local grocery store on my GPS to make sure I know the way. I have been gone for too long.

Now that I've had my eyes opened, it feels like I'm seeing Rosedale for the first time. On the bulletin board at the front of the grocery store I notice the flyer for an LGBTQ center in Midville, the next town over, among a poster for the winter production of *The Wizard of Oz* at the Rosedale Art Center, business cards for junk hauling services, and babysitting advertisements.

I load up on eggs, bread, beans, and butter, and add

some veggies and fruits my dad asked me to get in response to the text I'd remembered to send him earlier in the day. He'd also told me to get beer, so I grab a couple of things at random. After trying all through undergrad to become a beer drinker, I finally admitted to myself I hate the stuff, but my dad didn't get the memo. I linger over the baked goods, but nothing looks as tasty as the pecan bar Shay promised me sounds, so I skip it. I grab ice cream, though. It might be the dead of winter, but as far as I'm concerned, it's always ice cream season.

I get in line and see a text from Courtney.

> Did you have a chance to check in with the flower guy yet?

Oh, I checked in with the flower guy, I want to answer. I suddenly, and for the first time, wish she and I had the kind of relationship where I could mention flirting with Shay, maybe get her advice about meeting up with him tomorrow.

But we don't. So I don't.

> I did. He's on top of things. We just need the centerpiece number to give him.

I load my groceries onto the conveyor belt. The checker has a purple-dyed faux hawk and a trans pride pin next to their name tag, which reads Leaf.

I feel strange, like the person I am when I'm home is stuck in an imagined past, and the world's moved on without me. Why am I holding on so hard to this version of myself when it's not real?

For a moment, I imagine myself spitting out the

words to my parents tonight over dinner. I sigh, knowing I won't. I'd tell them if they asked me directly. I'd tell them if there was someone important to let them know about. But until either of those things happens, being this version of myself feels more comfortable, at least when I'm in Rosedale. After all, I'll be going back to Chicago soon, where I don't hide who I am. I don't flaunt it, either, but that's just not me.

If I hadn't met Shay yesterday, I wouldn't be thinking about this period.

Maybe I should pass on the pecan bars after all.

FIVE
SHAY

THURSDAY BEFORE BED, I double and triple check my alarm. I want to make sure I have time to swing by Beck's Cookie Counter in the morning before I open the shop. The entire day I'd wondered if the cute vet would find a reason to come in, but he didn't. I have to hope the lure of pecan bars is enough to bring him back.

Friday morning I first hit up Hot Brew, where I order a flat white and a sandwich for later from a sleepy-looking Meadow.

"You okay?" I ask.

"Yeah, just stayed up too late." She cracks her knuckles. "We on for game night tomorrow?"

"Oh, yeah. Great." I'd forgotten our bi-weekly game night is this Saturday.

"Hey, do you think we could do it at yours? Our landlord is replacing our kitchen sink, but he keeps running into issues. The place is a wreck, not to mention the water's been shut off to the kitchen for two days."

"Uh. My place is kind of cramped, but sure." I'll think of something.

While I'm waiting, I survey the people seated at Hot Brew's cafe tables and spot Rodney Greer, the owner of Rosedale Flowers and More. We touch base about once a month to go over the books, but he's a pretty hands-off boss, a widower with two grown kids who live out of state.

I walk up to his table. "Hi Rodney."

He looks up from his mug of black coffee, his bushy gray eyebrows raised. "Shay, hello. Sit down, son," he says, indicating the empty chair across from him with a gnarled hand.

"Okay." I sit and take in his lined face, which looks sort of gray. "Is everything all right, Rodney?"

"I'm glad to run into you," he says instead of answering my question. "There are some recent developments I wanted to talk to you about. You have time now?"

My stomach swoops. Developments doesn't necessarily sound good. "Sure, I have some time before I need to open the shop."

"Good. Here's the thing." He pauses and I think about all of the possible "things" that might come out of his mouth. He's firing me. He's going to turn the shop into a sporting goods store. He's decided to liquidate his assets and head to Vegas. "I'm making plans to move to North Carolina, near my daughter. And keeping the business will be too hard for me long distance."

My last guess wasn't that far off, it seems. I consider the implications of what he's said. I don't really get the difficulty of keeping the shop when I literally do everything necessary to keep it running. But maybe that should have been my clue that he's not exactly invested in it. Does he want to close?

"What does that mean for the shop?" I ask carefully.

"Well, I was thinking you might want to buy it from me."

"I would love to buy the shop, Rodney," I respond enthusiastically, letting my heart get ahead of my calculator. Being the official owner of the place I've poured my sweat into for eighteen months would be a dream. And here's Rodney saying it's a real possibility.

"The shop is one matter. But I'm talking about the whole building. Have you ever thought about being a landlord?" He takes a sip of his coffee. "The realtor I've been talking to says a commercial real estate company would snap it up in a minute, but I don't like the idea of some big outfit taking over the leases of the tenants. I was hoping someone local would take it on, keep it the way it is."

"Um." My mind races, wondering how much that parcel is worth. It almost doesn't matter, since I don't have the kind of money I'd need for a down payment on what amounts to practically an entire block. *But Mom and Dad do*, a traitorous voice in my head whispers.

"I know it's a lot to consider. And I hate to put pressure on you, but my daughter Janine really wants me down there by spring. I've had a few health problems, and it'll be easier on her if I'm nearby."

"Oh, Rodney. I'm sorry to hear that. I hope it's not serious."

"Just getting old. It's a privilege, they say." He smiles,

taking ten years off his countenance. "And a real pain in the ass."

I smile back. "Well, I'm sure your daughter will be glad to have you closer."

"The change of scene might be good for me," he says gruffly. "Plus the grandkids are a hoot. And since Rachel died, Rosedale doesn't feel as much like home as it used to."

He's mentioned his wife several times to me. The flower shop was her idea, back in the day.

Ruth brings my coffee to the table, lidless as usual. I lightly blow across the surface, wondering exactly how to ask him how this might work, how much he wants for the building, what will happen to the flower shop if I'm not able to buy it.

He looks out the window. "It's going to snow."

I take an awkward sip of my coffee, gazing at the gray sky. "I didn't know snow was in the forecast."

"Just flurries later," Rodney says. "But you never know. We haven't had a big snowfall yet this winter. They seem to come fewer and farther between."

Growing up, I only saw snow when we went to the mountains, but I never stopped finding it magical.

"But you don't have time to make small talk with an old man," Rodney says, his gaze returning to me. "Back to business."

"All right." I straighten in my chair, trying to look like a person who could possibly pull off buying commercial real estate.

"I talked to Noelle—she's the agent handling the vacant space next door to the flower shop. I haven't gone so far as to draw up a listing for the building, and if you buy it, I won't have to list it at all. You're good people, Shay. You're new to town, but you care about Rosedale. And I trust you to make the right decisions."

"Wow." I swallow against a wave of nerves. It's a lot of responsibility assigned to me by a guy I've known for less than two years. "I don't know what to say."

"I want you to have the flower shop. I'll sign it over to you for a buck," he says casually, as if he's ordering another coffee. It sounds too good to be true. Then he adds, "If you buy the building."

"And if I don't?"

"Well, we'll have to see. Look, the building can be yours for the low end of what Noelle says the place is worth." He names a price, a number larger than anything I've ever been involved with. I do some quick math in my head. My savings are definitely not enough. But maybe I could qualify for a loan.

"It's a tempting opportunity," I say, "and I'm honored that you'd want me to take on the responsibility. You know I love running the flower shop. It's really just a matter of finances. I have to figure out if I can swing it."

"You'll manage it," he says with certainty. "I wish I could let you have it for less, but Janine's right, it's basically my retirement. Who knows how long this ticker is going to keep going, but I could live for another couple of decades, and I'm not going to be a burden to my kids."

"I understand. I'll have to put some numbers together," I say. "What's the timeline for this?"

"Well, I don't want to rush you, but if I'm going to put it on the market, I have to be prepared that I won't find a buyer right away. Let's say I'd need an answer in...a month?"

It's soon, but I should be able to give him a yes or no in that time frame. That puts us right before the Valentine's rush. "Okay, Rodney. I'll see what I can do. Thanks for this opportunity."

He stands up, and I stand, too, offering him a hand, which he shakes gravely. "I have a good feeling about this, Shay."

I swallow my nerves and smile. "Have a good day, Rodney." Feeling dazed, I leave him at the table and swing by the counter where Ruth hands me my sandwich in a paper bag.

"You okay, Shay?" she asks in her small voice.

I shake myself. "I have no idea. I'll keep you posted." I've got to run the numbers, prep my orders for the day, open the shop. Oh—and get pecan bars. I blow a kiss to Meadow at the espresso machine, then carefully hold my lidless flat white while speed walking down the block to Beck's Cookie Counter, which thankfully opens an hour earlier than the flower shop. Beck himself is behind the register when I burst in.

"Please tell me you have pecan bars today." I gasp for breath, scanning the glass case for my quarry.

"Where's the fire, Shay?" Beck laughs. "I know my pecan bars are good, but they're not a cure for anything."

"Oh, it's not an emergency, I guess, unless curing my stunted love life counts."

Beck goes all fluttery. "Oh, I'm intrigued. And my baking can only help when it comes to love. You're in luck. I have a batch cooling in the back. How many do you need?"

They're huge and addictive and one each is probably enough but I'm not leaving anything to chance. "Four, please. Thank you."

"I got you. Anything for love!"

WHEN I GET BACK to the shop, I look around and imagine what it would be like to own the place. I know I already act like I do, but it's different actually being the one who's calling the shots, who's on the line to make payroll and pay taxes. The more I think about it, the more the responsibility seems it might be more than I'm ready for. Not to mention the additional burden of owning an entire building, with the associated maintenance and liability.

No wonder Rodney wants to give it up and retire for real.

But as I go through my day, munching on my sandwich and ringing up a sale of a sansevieria and a greeting card for a birthday present, the idea grows on me. I already know Rosedale is where I want to put down roots. Maybe this is exactly the opportunity I've been looking for.

Only how am I going to afford it?

SIX

CONNOR

"WHERE ARE YOU OFF TO?" Violet asks as I wind my gray scarf around my throat. We've finished our last appointment for the day. I've already changed out of my dirty work scrubs and washed up. Tara just left, and the cacophony of the day has ended, leaving only the low hum of the HVAC system.

"I'm not off anywhere," I say, even though that's unequivocally untrue. I'd hoped to be able to pop over to the flower shop on my lunch break, but I barely had time to scarf down my meal before an emergency patient got me back to work. It's a little after five now, but I'm hoping Shay will still be in the flower shop even though— according to my maps app—it closes at five on Fridays.

"Oh, I thought maybe you were meeting friends for dinner or something. Have you got in touch with any of your old buddies since you came back to town?"

"Uh, no. I've been busy."

"Good thing it's the weekend, then."

"I'm planning to catch up on sleep," I say, relieved to

be telling the truth this time. "What about you? You got big plans?"

"Your mother and I are working on the seating arrangements for the wedding. And I've got indoor pickleball on Sunday. Might catch a movie with some friends. The usual. Please don't spend the entire weekend sleeping. You're young, you should be having fun."

"In Rosedale?" I can't help sounding skeptical.

"I've had about enough of the negging, Connor Nieves. Rosedale may be small, but there's plenty going on. I think the Art Center has an event this weekend. Go to that. You'll see."

"I'll think about it." It occurs to me that if we leave at the same time, she's going to have more questions when I don't go directly to my car. "Uh. I'll lock up. You go ahead."

"All right. See you Monday if not before. Oh, and Connor?"

I pause and tilt my head in question.

"You did a great job this week."

"Thanks." I feel good about the work I did this week, but it's nice to hear that someone else thinks I did good, too. Being the only vet in a practice is a big responsibility. I have to show up and give 100% to every patient, which means I really am exhausted enough to sleep all weekend.

Violet exits to the parking lot, and I wait until I'm sure she's had time to drive away before I turn off the lights, set the alarm, and head out the back. It's gone dark, but the streetlights illuminate a light flurry of snowflakes, lending a magical air to the cold evening as I jog around the side of the building. It hasn't properly snowed yet this winter, and the hint of moisture has me feeling like a kid hoping for a snow day from school.

When I get to Rosedale Flowers and More, the door is locked, but the lights are still on. I squint through the window, but don't see Shay. Damn. Did I miss my chance?

I hesitate before knocking. Maybe this is for the best. Maybe I shouldn't have put myself out there even in this minor way. Forget the fact that I've been having a hard time not thinking about him since we met, that our inter-action the other day was the most exciting thing to happen to me in ages. Actually seeking him out means acknowledging a part of myself I'm used to ignoring when I'm here.

I huff out an exasperated breath. Violet was admon-ishing me for being too young to stay home, but I'm also too old to be afraid to go after something I want.

The question is, is spending more time with Shay something I want?

I raise my hand, tap on the glass loudly.

Well, that answers that.

A moment later, Shay appears from the back, catches sight of me, and makes his way to the door. He looks good. Today his hair's pulled back at the nape of his long neck, not at the top of his head. He's not wearing an apron the way he was the other day, so now I can see the full, long lines of his body. Standing next to him now without the counter between us, I can really feel the height difference—he's probably got almost half a foot on me.

I've always liked taller guys.

His shirtsleeves are rolled up to the elbows, revealing the sleeve of tattoos on his left arm. His other arm is tattoo-free, but he's got a collection of bracelets around that wrist, and a chunky silver ring on his middle finger.

"You made it." I can't tell from his tone if he's pleased or pissed, but he ushers me in and locks the door behind me, leading me to the counter with the register.

"Sorry it's on the late side," I say, unwinding my scarf in the humid warmth of the shop. "Busy day at work."

He tosses me a look over his shoulder, drags out two metal stools. "Lots of animals needed rescuing?"

"A few." I perch on one of the stools, then take off my coat. I start to wrap it under my arm, but he gently takes it from me without a word, laying it on a nearby table. "A few just needed their regular checkups and shots. Busy day for you?" The flower shop smells as amazing as it did the other day, and it looks like he was in the middle of putting together some kind of bouquet at the work table in the back near the refrigerated case of cut flowers.

"You have no idea," he says. "I'm glad you didn't come earlier because the afternoon had an unexpected rush. But I did procure us some pecan bars, if you're ready to get your mind blown." He produces a small brown box, takes the other stool, and offers me first pick of four large gooey-looking squares with a shortbread base, glistening filling, and studded with tempting chunks of pecans.

"These are big enough to spoil my dinner."

"What the hell, live a little. Dessert first once in a while won't kill us."

I laugh and take the top bar. "Death by pecan bar wouldn't be the worst way to go, anyway."

"Not if it's this pecan bar, honestly." He selects one, sets the box on the counter, and takes a bite. I'm about to take my own mouthful, but I'm caught up watching his eyes flutter shut as he moans, his pink lips gaining a hint of gloss as he chews. He looks better than the dessert, and I have the strongest urge to lick the flavor out of his mouth.

He opens his eyes and looks expectent. "What are you waiting for?"

I can't exactly say that watching him eat is turning me on, so I shove the bar in my face, snapping off a large piece. At the first touch to my tongue, I'm hit with a burst of caramelized brown sugar and nutty, buttery perfection.

"Mmmrgh." I make a noise around my full mouth.

"I know, right?" He smiles, pleased at my orgasm-adjacent response, and takes another bite.

I'm caught in the sensory overload of watching him eat, turned on by imagining him taking that much plea-sure in my body, or in him letting me attempt to satisfy him as much as the damn pecan bar. Meanwhile, it's the best thing I've ever eaten, and I finish the entire bar before I know what I'm doing.

"Shit." I'm breathing slightly noisily; it's kind of embarrassing how into that I was.

"I told you," he says smugly. "Beck's a genius."

The real reverence in his voice has me frowning. Is Shay into this cookie genius? Am I reading our pecan bar interaction all wrong? "You're friends with this Beck guy?" I can't help asking.

"Yeah, I guess. He's my friend Jack's cousin." Shay looks at me shrewdly. "And he's got a gorgeous boyfriend. Donovan Eastman, the actor?"

I shake my head. Doesn't ring a bell.

"Donovan mostly does theater—he's an honest-to-god Broadway star. But he's also involved in the local theater scene."

"Theater scene?"

"They're doing *The Wizard of Oz* in a couple of weeks. There's actually a fundraiser on Sunday over there for their kids' outreach program. I'm donating a basket to the silent auction." He nods at the work in progress at his bench. "You should donate something, if you can. Or—" He snaps his mouth shut.

"Or what?"

"I was going to say you could come with me to the event—bid on some items. It should be a good time." He looks at me carefully, as if gauging my reaction to the invitation.

I take a breath. Might as well be the adult I pretend to be. "Like...as a date?"

"Yeah," he says quietly, "if you want. Or just friends. If you want."

He's leaving it up to me, which is thoughtful. It's nice to know that he wants to hang out with me, even if it's not romantic.

Thing is, I'm honestly attracted to the guy. I have been since I first saw him. But making this a date means being a grownup in other ways, too.

"When on Sunday?" I ask to buy myself some time.

"Let's meet at five. In the winter, we do things early around here."

"Five," I repeat. Even though it makes my palms sweaty to commit, I can't think of anything I'd rather do than spend more time with Shay. "Pick you up here?"

"Are you a good driver?"

"Yes?" I am actually a good driver, but I'm not expecting the question.

"Oh, that's good. I live in fear of having to drive the shop's van in the snow."

"Is it supposed to snow?"

"No, but you never know."

He's so calm, cool, and collected—it's kind of sweet to see him unsettled about something. "Well, I'm driving my mom's SUV right now. It's got great traction."

"Perfect. So it's a date, then?" he asks.

Who would have thought I'd make a date with a guy as hot as Shay in *Rosedale*? "Yeah. It's a date."

He gives me a big smile that transforms his face from a cool marble carving into a warm wreath of creases.

"What car do you have in Chicago?"

"No car there. I stick to public transportation."

"That's cool. You have to have a car around here, though I don't drive if I can help it."

"How do you get to work?"

He smiles again, smaller this time, and points above him. "I live upstairs. I like to say I have Rosedale's shortest commute."

"Oh wow. That's cool." I swallow, thinking about the

possibilities now that I know his place is literally upstairs. That his bed is only steps away.

"It's not huge, but it works for me. Where do you live?"

"I'm staying with my parents. I even have my old bedroom."

"Did they keep it as a shrine to you?"

"God no. My folks aren't sentimental like that."

"Lucky. My parents still have all of my crayon drawings from kindergarten in archival boxes."

"Do they live nearby?"

His eyebrows rise in alarm. "No. They're back in Arizona."

"Arizona, huh?" I glance at his milky white complexion. "You don't strike me as a desert person."

"The sun and I are not friends," he agrees. "What about you?"

"I like the sun, but I've always liked winter, too."

"I hope so, given your last name. Nieves means snow in Spanish, right?"

I laugh. "Yeah. My dad's grandparents were from Spain, but he's a New Yorker born and bred. Married a Connecticut girl and they ended up here."

"Tú hablas español?" he asks with a perfect accent.

I laugh again, impressed. "Un poco. Tú?"

He shrugs. "It's hard to grow up in the southwest without learning some. I like languages."

"That's useful. I speak dog and cat, I guess, but I'm not that handy with anything besides English. Which works out, since my dad speaks even less Spanish than I do."

"They must be happy you're back at home."

"Yeah. Well, with the wedding coming up, it's helpful to have more hands on deck. And with my mom's arm the timing is good for me to be here for a while."

"But not to stay?" He asks it so mildly I could pretend to ignore the real question underneath it.

"I don't know," I say, wanting to be honest. "I don't have anything really pulling me back to Chicago—I had a temp job there. But a few days ago, I wouldn't have considered Rosedale a real option." I've been down on the town, but there was a time, long ago, when being a vet in Rosedale was my dream. Then I went through puberty, and everything got so much more complicated.

Oblivious to my ambivalence, Shay says, "I get it. Rosedale is tiny. But I like that about it."

"My mom's practice is surprisingly busy—though she is the only vet in town."

"Until now," Shay says.

We talk until I realize I either have to ask him if he wants to get dinner or say goodbye until Sunday and our official date. I'm surprised by how quickly the time passed, but it seems like a bad idea to press my luck. Instead we exchange numbers, and, despite my protests, he makes me take the leftover pecan bars.

I think about his words on the drive home, during which I'm unable to stop smiling. Rosedale does have another vet, at least for now.

SEVEN
SHAY

AFTER I SAY AN ABSURDLY reluctant goodbye to Connor and finish up the basket for the fundraiser, I text my brother.

> Hey. How are you and Jen? I have a business question when you have a minute to talk.

Tye calls when I'm making myself a chicken stir-fry for dinner while listening to a podcast explainer about commercial real estate.

"Hey, Tye Dye." I greet him with the nickname I came up with when I was an annoying seven-year-old.

"Hey Shady," he says, using his equally stupid nickname for me. Tye's given me a variety of nicknames over the years, but Shady's the one that stuck. I've always been weedy, but in high school I was nothing but arms and legs, and Tye started calling me Slim, then Slim Shady, then finally just Shady. Silly nicknames aside, he's a pretty decent big brother. He was the one who I came out to first, and he was unhesitatingly supportive, even staying by my side when I told Mom and Dad, who were fantastic. I don't think the news came as that much of a surprise to any of them, honestly, but we were all relieved after I made the implicit explicit.

"Everything good?" I ask.

"Work's good. I've been playing a lot of golf."

I shake my head, biting my tongue against a rant about how dry Arizona has no business maintaining golf courses. "What does Jen think about that?" Tye and Jen have been together since high school and got married a few years ago. She's an attorney, while he's followed in our parents' franchise footsteps.

"Actually, she's pretty pissed at me right now. She thinks we should get more serious about trying for a kid."

From the tone of my brother's voice I can tell he's not that enthusiastic about the idea. I turn the heat off under the stir-fry. "Oh. You don't think the time is right?"

"I don't know, it's just that having a kid will change literally everything about our lives. We'd talked about trying when we turned thirty, but I wasn't ready. She was cool with waiting a little longer, but now I think she's getting fed up."

"You still want kids, right?" I scoop rice onto a plate, add the veggies and some soy sauce.

"I mean, yeah. I always figured we'd have kids. Jen will be an awesome mom."

"That's a given," I agree. My sister-in-law is organized, caring, and has the patience of a saint to deal with my brother, even though that patience currently seems to be wearing thin. "You're going to be an awesome dad, you know."

Tye is silent for a beat. "You don't know that."

"I actually do. You were always there for me growing up. Always. And your own kid—you're going to love that kid so incredibly much. You just have to let yourself do it."

He blows out a noisy breath over the phone. "I don't know what's stopping me. I mean, things with Jen are good otherwise. I guess I should just get over myself. Anyway, what did you want to talk about?"

It's obvious that he wants to move the conversation off himself, but I said my piece and I really need his advice. "So an opportunity has come up," I say. "Or I think it has. Rodney, the owner of the flower shop, wants to sell me the business. But only as part of a bigger deal—he wants me to buy the entire building from him. Become a landlord. I'd love to own the shop, but owning a building? I don't know if I'm ready for that. Or if I could come up with enough money."

"Oh, wow. That's huge." He asks me a few practical questions about the flower shop's cash flow and profit and loss, then changes his tone. "Look, Shay, are you sure you want to invest in this town?"

"What do you mean?"

"I mean, why this place?"

"Rosedale?"

"Yeah, it's so random. We all thought it would last like six months and you'd be back in Scottsdale."

I bristle. His words aren't a surprise, but it's irritating to have to keep justifying my actions. "I like it here. It's a different way of life. You should come visit."

"Yeah, Mom mentioned something about that," he says. "But that's not the point. We miss you, dude. Your whole family is here."

"I know. I miss you guys, too." I do miss things about Arizona. But I love the life I'm carving out here.

"So let this guy find someone else to take over the business and come home. I'm sure Dad and Mom would give you money for a down payment on something here. You want to get into real estate? They'd be over the moon to help you out."

"If I did it in Scottsdale," I say, my voice flat.

"It just makes more sense," he says. "What kind of social life do you have there, anyway?"

I know he's asking out of love, but it's still insulting.

"I have friends," I insist. Maybe not as many as I had in Arizona, but through the power of the internet I still keep in touch with my best friends. Meadow and Melissa are such good friends I could call them in an emergency. Jack and Pete have become my friends, too. I got to know Jack when I was doing the flowers for their wedding last summer, and Pete's turned into a bit of a plant dad in the last few months. We spend time chatting about art or comics while I ring up his latest acquisition. There's Ruth at Hot Brew, and Beck at the cookie shop, and my regulars, like elderly Mrs. Kaufman who buys a bouquet every week to take to her sister in assisted living. I have plenty of friends.

"What about guys?" Tye presses. "You aren't still letting Ben get in your head, are you?"

Ben. My ex. The name I don't let myself think lest I start hyperventilating out of anger all over again.

So I just happened to have a messy breakup around the same time I found this job. So I just happened to move across the country instead of having to be reminded of the asshole who I thought I was in love with. So I just happened not to have gone on any real dates since Ben. Making out with tourists at Sparkle doesn't count.

"Look, I might have been running away when I came here," I acknowledge. "But Rosedale's grown on me. I like my job. It's not about Ben. Not anymore." I catch sight of the cute card Connor gave me peeking out of the top of my notebook. "Besides, I have a date Sunday."

"Really?" Tye's skepticism rankles. "Who with?"

"His name is Connor, and he's a veterinarian and he's very cute," I say with all the haughtiness I can muster.

"Well, that's great, Shady." Now he sounds... relieved? Like he was worried about me and the fact that I have an actual date with a real human man is reassuring news.

Has Tye had good reason to be concerned?

I guess I've been a little out in the cold here. Sharing pecan bars and going to a fundraiser with Connor is the slimmest of threads to hang my hopes on—Tye doesn't need to know that I barely know the guy. But he's a legitimate prospect. And even if there were no eligible men in a fifty-mile radius, I'd still want to invest in my future in Rosedale.

I steer the conversation back toward my initial question. "So besides asking Mom and Dad for money they aren't going to give me," I say, putting my personal life to the side, "what are my options?"

"Well, you're going to have to do some research and get some comp listings. You need to know how much rent you'll be able to collect. You could approach a bank, see how much they'd be willing to loan you. You have good credit, right?"

"I have excellent credit." It's not bragging if it's true. "So you think even though on paper my income is weak, a bank might take a chance?"

"You never know. It's a small town, right? Maybe they have a development program for locals. Doesn't hurt to ask."

I add "talk to someone at the bank" to my growing to-do list. "Okay. Thanks, Tye Dye."

"Let me know how it goes with Connor," he says warmly.

I feel bad for using Connor to placate my big brother's worrying.

"Sure," I say. "And you should probably talk to Jen. I know having kids is a big deal, but you're not going to figure anything out by avoiding her and playing golf."

He sighs. "Yeah. Okay. Talk to you later. Love you."

"Love you." I hang up, missing my brother with a startling ache. The last year and a half has allowed me to learn who I am away from my family, but at a cost. I look around my minuscule apartment, at my dinner for one. If I was back in Scottsdale, I'd be living on my own, too—there's nothing in the world that could induce me to live with my parents, even though they'd probably love it. But

Tye and Jen would be nearby—we'd get together for Sunday dinners and birthdays, and maybe I'll be an uncle sometime soon.

It's my turn to sigh. I stay up too late looking at interest rates and real estate listings, and when I finally sleep, I dream about Connor's lips, sticky and sweet.

BARRING an emergency call at the office, I have two whole days off stretching ahead of me. Courtney and Mike are doing a pre-marriage couples counseling retreat this weekend, and Dad's helping his clients get their 1099 forms out before the end-of-the-month deadline. Which means unless I want to hang out with my mom all day, I have to find something to do.

After breakfast, I work up a sweat on the treadmill, then find Mom in her office. She's scrolling through an article on her computer, her silvery blonde hair swept away from her lightly lined face.

"How's the arm?" I ask. She's got the injured one in her lap and she's awkwardly manipulating the trackpad with her non-dominant hand.

She glances over. "It doesn't hurt as long as I don't move it. Going to the doctor for a checkup Thursday."

"Well, I'm glad it's not bothering you too much."

"It's a nuisance," she says acidly. "I hate being away from the office. But Violet says things are going great," she adds, softening her voice. "You have any questions about anything? How was the Morrison poodle?"

"She's doing well. Her stitches will come out in a few days."

"And you got the order of Adaptil? Sometimes it gets delayed, and I have to call and yell at them."

I smother a smile. "As much as I know you'd love to have a reason to yell at someone, it arrived yesterday."

She gives me a look. "Well, it seems like you have everything under control."

High praise. "If Dad lets you, you should come by and see for yourself."

She gives me another look, one I know means Dad doesn't *let* her do anything.

"More reruns for you, then?"

"No, Violet's coming over and we're doing wedding stuff. You want to put your two cents in on the seating chart?"

I take two steps backward, my eyes widening in horror.

She laughs a little. "Okay, you have better things to do. I get it. Meeting up with some of your friends?"

"Maybe," I say noncommittally.

"Josh Ward was here at Christmas. He and his wife recently had a baby."

"Oh, good for them," I say, trying to drum up some enthusiasm for one of my old baseball teammates. Josh wasn't a bad kid, but he was the kind of boy who seemed to effortlessly fit in while it was a daily struggle for me to make sure I performed to expectation. And never, ever gave off a hint that I wasn't like the other kids. "Bye, Mom."

She looks as if maybe she wants to say something else, but then she waves me off with her non-broken arm. "Bye."

The flurries we got last night didn't turn into anything, so the roads are clear, but the sky is metal gray, as if all someone has to do is reach up and shake the flakes loose to set off an actual snowstorm.

I get in the car with no real destination in mind. I'd go to the flower shop to visit Shay, but we have a date tomorrow night—don't want to seem too desperate. It's sad I don't know anyone else in Rosedale. I haven't bothered to keep up with anyone here.

Then I remember I do know someone else in Rosedale, if the girl I took to prom a decade ago counts, and I point the SUV downtown. Today it's even harder to find a parking spot, so I'm forced to park on a side street and walk down the block, passing in front of a bookstore—small, but with a curated selection in the window that makes me want to find out what else they carry, so I pop in.

I browse the front shelves, wondering where this place was when I was growing up. The closest bookstore was at the mall a half hour drive away. Courtney and I spent a lot of time at the library, but there's nothing like the intoxicating scent of new books and being able to take them home to keep.

I've been too distracted to read much lately, but normally I enjoy unwinding with procedural thrillers and spy stories, and I grab a couple by authors I like. There's a rack of greeting cards by the register and I idly page through them.

The woman crouched down behind the register stands up, a tape dispenser in her hand. "Hello," she greets me pleasantly. "All set?"

"Hi," I say, recognizing her as the woman who kissed Meadow at Hot Brew yesterday. Should I say something?

"Oh, I know you," she says brightly. "Meadow mentioned a high school friend of hers was in town—it's Connor, right?"

"That's me," I say, slightly shocked by Meadow calling me a friend, but at the same time, warmed by the description. "Connor Nieves."

"I'm Melissa Sanchez," she says. "I'm going to guess you aren't a member of the bookstore's rewards program."

"No, but I'd like to be," I respond, because why not? She smiles and walks me through joining, then rings me up.

"Meadow said you two went to prom together," Melissa says, sounding amused.

"True fact," I say. "My cummerbund even matched her dress."

"You wouldn't happen to have any photographic evidence, would you?" Melissa asks with a wicked smile. "I can't imagine Meadow in prom attire, and she swears she doesn't have any pictures. But I have to see this."

There's a photo album on the bookshelf in my parents' living room that I'm eighty percent positive contains prom pictures.

"I might be able to come up with some," I say, not quite sure if I should align so quickly with Melissa. If things are serious between them, then it probably won't hurt. "How long have you two been together, if you don't mind my asking?"

"Three years—well, four this summer," she says, smiling broadly. "We're really lucky."

I swallow against an unexpected lump in my throat. "Yeah. That's great," I say sincerely. "I'll see what I can do about the photo. You know, Meadow did me a solid by going as my date. She's a good person."

Melissa looks at me, her face now serious. "High school's not easy for anyone, is it?" she says. "I was a hot mess, that's for sure."

I offer her a close-mouthed smile. "It gets better, right?" I say, knowing she knows what I mean. And it did get better, but being home reminds me that I've missed out on making it better with those closest to me. At every turn, it feels like the universe is knocking me over the head with the fact that I just need to tell my family already and get on with my life.

"Yeah, it does." She cocks her head at me. "So, Connor, what are you doing later?"

"Um."

"'Cause Meadow and I are getting together with a couple of friends for game night—you know, dorky board games, bottle of wine? We usually get pizza or something. You should come. And you don't have to bring the prom photo—unless you want to," she adds with an evil-villain arched eyebrow.

"That's—" I have to fight a sudden, embarrassing well of tears, reminding myself that Nieveses don't cry. I take a steadying breath. "That's a really nice invitation. Sure. Sounds good."

"Oh great," she says with real enthusiasm. "Let me put your number in my phone and I can text you where to meet us. Meadow and I usually host but our landlord is doing 'improvements,'" she uses air quotes, and I laugh, "and I think we're doing it at our friend's. So I'll text you. Yay. This is going to be fun, Connor."

My phone buzzes with her text and I save her number. "Cool," I say, slightly bewildered by the turn of events, but happy. "See you later, I guess."

She waves at me cheerfully and I leave with my books in a canvas tote bag with the phrase "I like big books and I cannot lie" emblazoned on the side. I'm feeling a little shy about going to Hot Brew now, in case I run into Meadow again, but I remind myself that was the point of this excursion. Still, when I spot the bright blue and orange sign for Beck's Cookie Counter, I'm relieved to be able to duck inside.

The place is small and homey, with familiar alt rock playing over the sound system, the scents of brown sugar and chocolate and some kind of spice in the air. There's a kid-size table at one end of the room, where three little kids are coloring with crayons and munching on sugar cookies, with two women supervising while they sit and chat at the nearby blue high-topped counter.

A young woman and a young man are talking behind the counter, both sporting official-looking aprons. The woman wears chef's whites under hers, while the man has on a blue henley and jeans. She takes notes on a pad as the guy counts something off on his fingers.

"Six batches of oatmeal raisin, four of the double chocolate, and two sugar. And we better triple the pecan this week. We sold out in about an hour yesterday."

"Got it," the woman says.

"Thanks, Sabrina," he says, and the woman disappears in the back while he turns his attention to me. "What can I get for you?"

"Did I hear you're sold out of the pecan bars?" I say. "I had one yesterday, and it was honestly the best thing I've ever put in my mouth."

The guy smirks. "I'm going to take that as a compliment and not as an indictment of your love life."

I burst out with a shocked laugh, and the smirk falls from his face. "Sorry—inappropriate, I know. Forget I said that. My boyfriend's always telling me I'm going to scare away customers with my lack of filter. But then again, it's my shop, so I can sort of say what I want. What did you want again?"

"No, it's okay," I say, smiling at the guy, who must be Beck, the owner. "Sadly, both are true. But if I can't get those, what do you recommend?"

"Wait—pecan bar?" He looks at me more carefully. "Did you get this pecan bar from Shay Brierley?"

"Yeah," I admit, hoping the mention of Shay doesn't bring a flush to my cheeks. "They were mind-blowing."

"Of course they were," Beck says pertly. "But we're out at the moment. So if *nuts* are your thing," he adds with a friendly leer, "you have a couple of choices. There's the flourless chocolate walnut cookie, or the trail mix cookie, which has a bit of everything: coconut, pumpkin seeds, dried cranberries, chocolate chips, and even pecans."

"Sounds hearty," I say. "I'll take a couple of those."

"You got it—oh." Beck puts a hand to his cheek. "But if you're getting one for Shay, I'd recommend something else. He hates coconut." He waits for me to confirm or deny.

"Good to know," I say, trying to keep my voice neutral. "But I'm not getting one for him."

If Beck's disappointed at my discretion, he doesn't show it. "Okay. What else sounds good?"

I scan the case and see sugar cookies, iced ones in the shape of snowflakes. "My sister Courtney ordered some sugar cookies for her wedding—are those the same kind?"

"Ah yes, the Valentine's Day wedding," Beck answers with a snap of his fingers. "Yep, those are them. My staff will be working overtime to fill that order. Normally I love weddings, but even though this is our first Valentine's Day with the shop open, I have a feeling it's going to be a busy week."

"Makes sense." I never thought about the timing of Courtney's wedding. It's cool that she's using so many local vendors, though. And sugar cookies seem like a safe bet to bring to game night later. Melissa hadn't said to bring anything—blackmail fodder against her girlfriend aside—but I don't want to arrive empty-handed. "I'll take half a dozen of those, too."

"You got it." He puts six crystalline sugar cookies in a brown box and slips the trail mix cookies into a separate bag, then totals me up. "So you're Courtney's brother. Are you in the wedding party?"

"Connor," I say, offering a hand, which Beck shakes. "I'm a groomsman, yeah."

"You have a wedding date? Not asking for me—I'm taken," he says quickly, "but Shay would make a very good plus-one."

I shake my head. Jesus. Do I have gay stamped on my forehead? How can all these nice queer Rosedale people see it and my family is so oblivious?

But then what Beck's implying sinks in, and my face heats for real. "Shay's really, uh, great," I say haltingly. "We're actually going to some fundraiser thing tomorrow," I add, proud of our date.

"Oh, at the Art Center?"

When I nod, Beck grins. "Awesome. It's going to be a fun night. My boyfriend Donovan teaches acting classes at the Art Center. He's donating some Broadway tickets to the silent auction, so bring your credit card."

"Will do. Okay, well, I'll see you then, I guess."

Beck claps his hands together happily. "Fantastic. More friends."

I back out of the shop, wondering if I've actually made two friends by simply shopping. Is that a win for capitalism? The sky got darker while I was inside, and I munch on a trail mix cookie—delicious—in lieu of lunch. I haven't had such a nice day in recent memory. It's not like I go around Chicago making new friends all the time. In fact, most of my friends scattered after we finished our DVM program, going where the jobs were or moving to where their significant others wanted to settle. I didn't have anyone, or anything, to move for, so I stayed. But I hadn't realized how lonely I've been. This return to Rosedale has certainly thrown all of that into relief.

I imagine a future where I stay here, with the nice friendly queers and the yummy cookies and the cute bookshop. What would I do—stay on at the veterinary office? Work with my mother?

I shiver at the thought of actually working alongside her, but I'm not sure if it's out of fear or excitement. Aren't they sort of the same thing?

She'd have to want me there. It's juvenile, but maybe what I've been doing by staying away has been to reject her, to reject this town, before it could reject me first.

NINE
SHAY

SATURDAY IS busy in the shop, the kind of day where I wish my budget for part-time help extended beyond events. At one o'clock I scarf down a sandwich standing up, and then I'm making two special orders in between dealing with customers the rest of the afternoon.

Just as I'm locking the door at five on the dot, Meadow's text arrives and makes me groan.

Game night at yours, right? Pete's busy so Jack wants in. I'll order the pizza. Melissa's getting wine and bringing a friend. See you in thirty.

I honestly have no idea how Meadow thinks we can fit five people in my shoebox of an apartment. Then I glance at the big table on the side of the shop, and realize if I clear it off and bring chairs from upstairs, we'll have enough.

> Let's do it in the shop. More room. See you soon.

I run upstairs, grab some paper plates and napkins, a few glasses from the motley crew of them I bought at the secondhand store when I first moved here, and my double fifteen dominoes set.

While I clear the table, moving the spider plants and philodendrons to a temporary shelf, my mind returns to Rodney's proposal that I not only take over the shop but buy the entire building. I've thought it over and buying the entire building would actually be financially smart for me. I wouldn't have to pay myself rent for the flower shop, and I'd have the income from the three other units to cover the mortgage and expenses, assuming I can find a tenant to fill the empty storefront. I'd have to learn how to maintain a commercial building and deal with tenant issues, but I'm pretty sure the upsides of potential profit and the satisfaction of owning a piece of Rosedale would be worth it.

But it all comes back down to actual dollars. Even if Rodney gives me a great deal, I have to come up with a lot of cash for the down payment, assuming a bank will give me a loan in the first place. What if I can't figure it out and some faceless corporation buys the building instead? Even if Rodney was willing to sell me just the flower shop, I'd never be able to suddenly afford rent on both the shop and the apartment. I'd have to move, maybe get a nine-to-five job instead of essentially being my own boss. Rosedale Flowers and More would probably close. I've sunk so much into this place that the idea of suddenly losing it all makes me itchy with anxiety.

Forcibly, I push aside these worries for another time. It's Saturday night, I have a day off tomorrow, and I have a date with a cute boy to look forward to. Tonight will be about unwinding with my friends and gorging myself on pizza.

Jack arrives first, tapping on the front glass, wrapped in a puffy ski jacket and green woolen hat that matches his eyes. He gives me a hug and hands me his offering of a veggie plate that clearly came from the grocery store's prepared foods section.

"Oh, thank god it's warm in here," Jack says, shivering. "It's not snowing, but it kind of feels like snow, you know? Hey, is this new?" he says, taking a look at a big dracaena with thin long leaves I put in a place of honor by the register earlier today.

"Yeah. Isn't it pretty?"

"Pete would love it."

"Where is your better half?" I ask.

"He's doing some last-minute stuff for tomorrow's event at the Art Center." He takes off his coat and hat, leaving his thick dark blond hair mussed. "You're coming, right?"

"I'll be there. The shop's donating some things to the auction. And I have a date," I add, a bit smugly.

Jack's eyes light up. I knew that would pique the interest of his romantic, gossip-loving heart. "A date? With whom?"

Suddenly, I feel jittery with nerves. Is it too soon to get this excited? We've only had two in-person interactions, after all. But it's been so long, I can't help but want to experience all the joy I can from anticipating seeing him again, this time when we've used the actual d-word.

"His name is—Connor!" I finish my own sentence with an exclamation of surprise.

Because it is Connor, in the flesh, walking through my door with Melissa and Meadow right behind him. He's carrying a Cookie Counter box, Melissa has an armful of wine, and Meadow's bringing up the rear holding two enormous pizza boxes.

"Uh, hi, Shay," Connor says, smiling sheepishly at me. "Melissa invited me to game night. I didn't know it was here."

"Wait, you two know each other?" Melissa glances between us, then exchanges a surprised look with her girlfriend.

"We met the other day," I say. I can't seem to help the growing smile on my face at seeing him again. We'd so carefully arranged our next meeting, but there's no script for this, and I suddenly don't know how to approach game night—it's not a date, is it? Is he just a friend of a friend in this situation?

It doesn't seem as if Connor knows quite what to do, either, as he sets the cookie box on the table, waves awkwardly to Jack, and takes off his peacoat.

"Well, we met today," Melissa says, plopping down two bottles of red and a bottle of white. I'm about to run back up to my place for a wine opener, but she fishes one out of her pocket. "But these two," she indicates Meadow and Connor, "go way back."

"Oh, yeah?" I need to know more, but my manners intercede. "By the way, Connor, this is Jack Avery."

Connor offers Jack a hand, and it's so interesting to watch him interact with other people. On the surface, he seems like a confident guy. I mean, he's a veterinarian—he had to have confidence to get through that gauntlet, I assume. But I can tell there's a vulnerability underneath. It's like he's holding something back. Maybe he's just shy until he gets to know someone.

"We went to high school together," Meadow says as if it's the most banal fact in the universe, but Melissa leans in and adds excitedly, "They went to *prom* together. Did you bring it?" she asks Connor.

His face reddens, and he turns to Meadow with an apologetic grimace. "Yeah. Sorry about this, Meadow."

She shakes her head as if disappointed in him, but then she says, "It's okay. I try not to have regrets in life. Show them." Then, belying her words, she puts her face in her small, chapped hands while Connor pulls a glossy 4x6 photo from his back pocket.

The rest of us crowd around him and I glimpse a slight fresh-faced version of Meadow, one with tawny hair and an electric blue ball gown with a full skirt and ruched bodice.

"Oh my gosh, babe. You look like Prom Barbie," Melissa says. I can't quite interpret her tone. Is she shocked? Impressed?

My gaze lands on Meadow's date, a shyly smiling eighteen-year-old Connor. His face is thinner, he hasn't yet filled out like he is today, but the hair is the same—thick on top and cut closer on the sides. He's wearing a slightly-too-big tux with a blue tie and cummerbund that match Meadow's dress. They're posed in front of an attractive white colonial-style house, not touching.

They look, frankly, like deer in the proverbial headlights, and my heart suddenly aches for these kids, who were trying to take part in a school ritual that didn't make room for them to really be themselves.

"Wow," I say lightly. "Those were the days."

"You couldn't be cuter, Connor," Melissa says, cooing. "Did you guys have fun?"

Connor glances at Meadow and puts the photo on the table. "We did, actually."

"Yeah, it was a pretty fun night," Meadow agrees.

"I'm in shock seeing you in an actual color, Meadow. You even wore black to my wedding," Jack says, reaching for the first pizza box. "Anyone mind if I crack this open?"

"Go for it," I say. "Oh, I love their sausage."

"Is there—oh great, veggie," Connor says when he checks the second box.

Something occurs to me. "Wait—are you a vegetarian?"

Connor smiles. "Mostly. I eat fish and dairy. But yeah, I stay away from meat and poultry. Kind of goes with the animal lover thing."

I look guiltily at the piece of sausage pizza on my paper plate. I've always been a big meat eater—my metabolism needs a constant supply of protein.

"Hey, no worries," he says lightly. He smiles at me over the open veggie pizza box, and my guilt fades away as butterflies take over. He really is awfully cute, and he chooses a seat that has an empty one next to him, so I take it, forcing Jack to sit at the end of the table on a stool. There's a flurry as everyone grabs pizza and pours liberal tumblers of wine.

Melissa whispers something in Meadow's ear; her cheeks pink up under her makeup. I spy them linking hands under the table and get a pang of envy. I want what they have someday. And while it's way too soon to say Connor is the one, it's nice to have a prospect.

"So you grew up in Rosedale, too," Jack says to Connor. "I haven't seen you around, though."

"I left a while back for school," Connor explains. "But my mom needed some help at her veterinary practice, so I'm here for a bit."

"Wait—your mom is Dr. Nieves?" Jack looks like Connor just said his mom was Taylor Swift. "We take our dog to her. She's amazing. Best vet I've ever had."

Connor smiles at the compliment. "She is an excellent vet."

"And you're joining her practice? That's so cool."

"Not exactly. She broke her arm, so I'm the fill-in."

I frown at the reiteration that he's only here temporarily. I knew that, but I'd shunted the fact to the back of my brain while the rest of me focused on his pretty mouth and dark eyes.

"Oh my gosh, well, tell her get well soon from me and Pete and Cleo—she's our dog."

"Will do," Connor promises.

"We don't have any pets—we rent—but all our friends with pets go to your mom, too," Meadow says. "They all say she's the absolute best."

"Big shoes to fill, for sure," Connor says a bit awkwardly.

I decide to rescue him. "You guys want to play dominoes?"

"Perfect," Meadow says. "Whatever requires the least brainpower. I'm fried after this week."

"I don't think I know how to play," Connor says.

"It's super easy." I sketch out the house rules for Mexican train dominoes and he nods along. We clear the food and drinks to the register counter and dump the dominoes onto the empty table with a raucous clatter.

"So I guess you had to go to school for a long time to become a vet?" Jack asks while we turn the dominoes face down.

"Four years at the University of Illinois Chicago after undergrad at Northwestern," Connor confirms.

Jack whistles. "Chicago, huh? You like it there?"

"It's okay," he says vaguely. "Cold winters."

"Well, Rosedale is happy to have you back," he says. "Even temporarily." He glances between the two of us curiously. "How did you meet again?"

"My sister's getting married in a few weeks—" Connor starts.

"And I'm doing the flowers," I finish, as if that explains everything.

Jack smiles uncertainly. "Okay."

Connor surprises me by elaborating. "And then Shay told me about your cousin's cookie store and the famous pecan bars."

"Damn, those things are good," Melissa says.

"And one thing led to another," Connor goes on.

"And then I think Shay asked me out." He looks at me, eyes wide, as if surprised by his own directness.

"I definitely asked you out," I agree, tossing him a reassuring smile.

"Now we're getting somewhere," Jack says. "Asked you out on a date?"

"Don't get your expectations up. We're going to a fundraiser together tomorrow," I say, talking to both Jack and Connor. "It's not dinner and a show, it's finger food and a silent auction."

"Oh, even better. Civic engagement and romance, I love it," Jack says. "Pete, my husband, teaches art classes at the Art Center sometimes. He's on the board now, so we have to go to everything."

"Like you wouldn't be there anyway," Meadow says. "Jack is Mr. Rosedale."

"I like it here," Jack says mildly. "I can't help it if everyone who comes to visit me falls in love with the town and wants to abandon everything to become a Rosedalian."

"Rosedalian?" I say, wrinkling my nose.

"It's something my friend Charlie came up with. Right before he decided to live here full time."

"It sounds kinda like a shrub," I say, turning the word over in my mind. "I like it."

"I think it makes us sound like creatures floating alone on our own little island," Meadow says.

"An island of joy," Melissa interjects teasingly.

"Oh, definitely," Meadow says. I can never quite tell if she's being sarcastic or not. But she's lived here longer than any of us, so I'm assuming she actually likes the place.

"Mr. Rosedale?" Connor asks. "Is that an official title?"

"Not yet," Jack says. "But maybe I should get business cards made up."

Everyone laughs. "Let's play," I suggest. Our version of dominoes isn't complicated—it's easy to learn but hard to win—and Connor catches on quickly.

Melissa wins the first game, but after we break out the sugar cookies he brought, Connor comes out on top in the second. After setting down the winning tile, he turns to me, face lit up like a Christmas tree. "I won!"

"You did." I laugh and have the strongest urge to kiss him. I sort of lean in, then pull back—it would be weird to have our first kiss in front of my friends. But is it my imagination or is his gaze tracking my lips with interest?

That's when I realize I've drunk more than my share of the wine and my head's a little swimmy. Thank god I don't have to open the shop tomorrow. There's still work to do, but I won't be constantly interrupted by customers.

"Well, I need to get this prom queen home," Melissa says, her arm around Meadow's waist.

"Hey, is it snowing?" Jack says, peering through the front windows. "It is—it's totally snowing."

We crowd around the window, and there is indeed a thin sheen of white over the sidewalks and street, at least what we can see in the light of a nearby streetlamp. It looks like a giant passed by, sifting powdered sugar onto everything.

"Damn. Now we really need to get home. Jack—

Connor—you good to drive?" After receiving affirmative responses, Melissa and Meadow wave goodbye. Then Jack looks up from his phone. "Pete's already home. He says the roads aren't bad yet. Connor—a pleasure to meet you, even if you beat me at dominoes. We'll have a rematch soon. And I'll see you two tomorrow?"

We nod, then he's gone, and it's just me and Connor.

"Guess I better get going," he says, shuffling his feet.

"Probably," I say. "Or—"

"Or?" He latches onto the word eagerly, and anticipation blossoms in my gut.

"Or you could stay for a little while. Or a long while."

TEN

CONNOR

"I CAN STAY FOR A LITTLE WHILE," I say, my heart immediately racing at Shay's pleased smile. What-ever music had been playing when I got here has died off and the shop is quiet and still without the commotion of the others.

"Great. More wine?" he asks.

I drank a couple of glasses while we ate pizza and played dominoes. "No thanks. Do you have any water?"

"How about some tea?"

"Even better."

"It's upstairs," he says, searching my face for an answer.

I only hesitate for a second. "Lead the way."

His smile grows. "Can you grab that bottle?"

I pick up the empties and the remaining half-full bottle of red. He collects the tumblers we'd used for wine glasses, double checks the front door is locked, but leaves the dominoes scattered on the table in the trains we made during the last game. I'm still excited about pulling off a win. Meadow had been really close and the dirty look she gave me when I set down my final tile was priceless.

"Should we clean up the game?"

"I'll get it tomorrow. The shop is closed on Sunday."

I follow him up a set of back stairs. This unit is constructed differently from the vet office; next door the back stairs lead to a modest set of rooms that Mom uses for old patient files and extra storage. But Shay's stairs lead to a cozy apartment with an efficiency-style kitchen, a round kitchen table with two chairs, and a living room dominated by a small couch. I can see a door to what must be the bedroom, and another to a bathroom, and that's the extent of the place.

I put the wine bottles on the kitchen table, then wander into the living room half of the space. There are a couple of bookshelves that hold some books, yes, but also plants. Lots and lots of plants. Two rectangular grow lamps hanging from the ceiling provide extra light and lend the place an otherworldly glow.

"You look like you need a greenhouse," I say, gesturing to the seedlings and cuttings.

"Someday," he says. "But this is the best I can do for now." He sets down the glasses in the sink and toes off his shoes, then fills an electric kettle and flips the switch. "Is chamomile okay?"

"Perfect."

"You wanna get more comfortable?" he asks gently, and I realize I'm just standing in the middle of his living room with my coat under my arm.

"Sure," I say, trying not to sound as nervous as I feel. I order myself to get it together. I'm acting like I've never been alone with a guy, which is ridiculous. I've been with lots of guys—well, a fair amount. But this is different. This isn't an app hookup, or a friends-with-benefits situation like I had with a couple of guys back in school. This is someone I actually like. A guy who pushes my buttons and—miracle of miracles—seems to like me back. Someone I see possibilities with.

Admittedly, those possibilities also kind of scare me. Because being with someone who matters to me means opening up in a way I've protected myself from doing my entire life.

I set my coat down, take off my shoes quickly, leaving me in thick dark wool socks just like Shay's. When he comes to hand me a steaming mug of tea, I notice his feet are quite a bit bigger than mine.

"Thanks," I murmur, taking the mug.

"Let's sit," he says, sinking down on the couch, blowing on the surface of his tea.

"I hope it wasn't weird that I showed up tonight—Melissa honestly didn't tell me that her game night crew included you. When she texted me the address, it felt too late to back out."

He cocks his head at me. "Would you really not have come if you'd known?"

"Maybe not. I wouldn't have wanted to seem like I was stalking you."

He smiles. "Small town," he says, as if that explains everything. "I'm glad you came. It was fun. Though I still can't believe you and Meadow went to prom together."

I laugh. "It makes so much sense in retrospect, but at the time, I had no idea she was queer."

"Did you know you were queer?" he asks me quietly.

"Yeah," I say. It's so much easier to talk about this stuff with someone who just lays it all out there. "But I was panicked about it. And I knew taking someone to prom would make my parents happy, so when Meadow asked me, it was a huge relief. We weren't super close friends, but we honestly ended up having fun. She's pretty great, underneath that crusty exterior."

"I know. We go to Sparkle sometimes, and if there's karaoke—watch out."

"What's Sparkle?"

He chuckles. "Man, you really are from out of town. Sparkle is the gay bar in Midville. It's decent."

Midville has a gay bar. My high school prom date is a lesbian. I got picked up by a hot florist within forty-eight hours of coming home.

"Okay, so I'm officially over my Rosedale sucks stance," I confess. "I can admit when I'm wrong, and I clearly stayed away too long."

"Jack will be so happy to hear it," Shay says. "How's your tea?"

I take a sip of the warm brew. It's delicate and delicious. "Really good."

"Yeah?" He looks pleased. "I made it myself from chamomile I harvested late last summer."

"Impressive," I say. "You're an herbalist, too?"

"A budding one," he says, and I laugh. "Pun not intended."

"Right." I take another sip, the drink warming my belly pleasantly. "So, did you go to prom?"

"I did go to prom, but in a big friend group. None of

us had it together to get actual dates, plus I didn't feel like making a big statement or anything by going with a boy. It was easier to be in a group. It was pretty anticlimactic. You hear all through high school how special prom is supposed to be and then it just turns out to be an expensive dance with people barfing in the bushes."

"Totally. Were you out, then?"

"Oh yeah," he says, blasé. "I was out to my family when I was like thirteen, and I think everyone in school knew by the time sophomore year rolled around."

"Wow. Was that hard?"

"Sometimes. But mostly it was good. I never felt like I had to be someone else, at least not more than the average high schooler does."

It strikes me what I've found so appealing about Shay since we met. "I think you're really good at being yourself."

He digests the comment and acknowledges it with a nod. "Thank you. You know, when I came here, it was really the first time I'd truly been on my own. My parents, my brother, my friends, they were always my safety net. And I know I still have them and their support, but it's been a good experience getting to know what I'm capable of when it's just me."

"And you already have a good friend group here."

"Well, Melissa and Jack made it easy for me. They kind of made me be their friend. They're natural connectors. Beck, too."

"I noticed. I walked down Main Street and tripped over two new friends."

"That's Rosedale for you," Shay says.

I laugh into my tea. "Don't small towns have a reputation for being backwards and judgy?"

"Some of them are. But small towns also have a way of pulling people into the fabric of the community."

"Whether they want to be pulled or not?"

"Maybe." Shay looks at me over his mug, his eyes reflecting the grow lights. "Maybe the community sees people who need a place and opens its arms to them."

Did I ever have a community like that in Chicago? I had my college friends, my vet school class, some of whom I got pretty close to. But the longer I stayed in academic life, the less the wider community seemed to be something I could break into. And when school ended and everyone went their separate ways, I was the only one left.

"Well, I don't know if I'm a good fit for Rosedale, but I appreciate the gesture," I say.

"Tonight was fun," Shay says, his tone changing. He sets his mug on the coffee table with half a dozen baby succulents on it. "Do you want to hear something funny?"

"What's that?"

"I wanted to kiss you like three times tonight. But I thought it would be weird if our first kiss was in front of everyone else."

My stomach leaps. I admire how casually he throws that out there and thrill at how his words match exactly how I was feeling. It had been strange to sit next to him all night but not touch. Not that we've touched all that much. But for a not-date, it felt kind of date-y. And Melissa and Meadow were touching each other all night, small pats to the shoulder, quick pecks to the lips. At one point, Meadow stroked Melissa's cloud of hair, and I glanced over at Shay, wanting to know what his long hair felt like. Is it as soft as it looks?

But I couldn't find out, because Shay's right. "First kisses should be in private," I murmur. I deliberately set my tea down next to his, then scoot forward on the couch.

He immediately moves to meet me in the middle, catching me when I sway toward him and lose my balance. He puts his hand on my shoulder and his mouth on mine. His lips are warm from the tea. I tilt my head, changing the angle, and his mouth tastes floral when he opens up to me.

We pull away at the same time. His face is still close, letting me see where his blond eyelashes turn dark at the roots, a small mole on the edge of his left eyebrow I never noticed before.

The hand on my shoulder drops away, and he leans back. "Okay?"

"Very okay," I assure him. "First kiss, check."

He chuckles. "Well, I hope it was more than something to check off your list."

"It's only the beginning," I say, finally confident. I've always liked kissing, and the sex part of relationships has invariably been where I'm the least constrained. I can turn off my brain, let my body do the work. Sex is maybe where I feel the most like myself—where my outward inhibitions drop away and I'm free. Free to experience, free to act.

"That sounds promising," he says—but then he rocks back, just out of reach. "What about the snow?"

"Snow?" I repeat blankly. Oh right, snow. I totally forgot about the weather.

He gets off the couch, stoops as the ceiling drops the closer he gets to the low-set window that overlooks Linden Street. He shifts the old-fashioned blinds to survey the outside. "It's still coming down."

I follow him to the window, tucking my body close to his, but not quite touching. He's bent down so I can easily peer over his shoulder to see for myself that it is indeed still snowing, maybe half an inch more since we last checked. I can see my mom's SUV parked on the street below where I left it earlier that evening, coated in snow. "Oh. Well, they might plow."

He hums, doesn't turn around. "Maybe you should stay until they get the roads cleared."

I tense. Is this an invitation to spend the night? "You don't mind putting me up?"

He turns around now, stands to his full height, and I step back to give him space as he searches my face with his gaze. "You want to sleep over?"

I do, but I'm not sure what that would mean to him, exactly. "Yeah, but we don't have to—"

He talks over me. "Here's the thing—" He stops.

I wait for him to go on, and when he doesn't, I prompt. "What?"

He huffs out a breath. "If you stay over, I'm going to want to—" He puts a hand on my hip, tips his forehead down to mine. I easily get the picture.

"That's not a problem," I promise.

"Yeah?" He brushes my lips with his. "Not too fast?"

I shake my head. "We've already gone slower than I do with most of the people I sleep with."

He puts more space between us. "Oh." He looks suddenly uncertain, and I know I said something wrong.

"Flirting, making dates, game night—all the stuff we've done so far—I'm not very experienced with all that. I've never really had a relationship that started like this. So I don't really know how good of a job I've been doing. But sex—I'm good at that."

He cracks a smile. "Did you just tell me you're good at sex?"

"Yeah." I swallow. Oh shit. I *am* good at sex, aren't I? I think back to the last time I did it—with Nico, my former org chemistry lab partner who'd just broken up with his boyfriend and wanted a quick rebound fuck. I was happy to oblige, and he was not faking his enthusiasm for the physical stuff, even if his heart was nowhere near the bedroom.

"Yeah," I say with more confidence. "You wanna see?"

"I really do," he says, and then we're kissing again, the snow falling silently outside, the thump of my heart drowning out any noise inside Shay's apartment.

ELEVEN
SHAY

CONNOR EXCUSES himself to use the bathroom, and I take a minute to compose myself. I started this day thinking it would be a normal Saturday and am ending it with a cute boy guaranteeing me good sex. It's a lot to take in.

I bring our now cold teas to the kitchen sink, switch off the light, check the door's locked, and go to my room. I turn on the lamp next to my bed, shake out the quilt, sniff the air. It doesn't smell bad, but I light a candle, one we sell in the shop, that smells like mown grass to freshen things up.

I check the carved wooden box next to the lamp for supplies. I have some condoms in there, even though I haven't needed them since I moved here. The lube is fresh, because that comes in handy, so to speak, all the time. I don't have toys—I'm sort of boring that way.

It's only then, when I'm sitting on the edge of my bed contemplating if I should take off any of my layers, or any jewelry, that I realize I'm nervous.

When it was flirting in the shop and pecan bars and dominoes, it was easy to keep it light and fun and low stakes. But now Connor's going to spend the night, and we're going to have sex the same night as our first kiss.

And okay, to be fair, I've had sex with people I never even kissed at all—it happened once or twice at parties—and I've kissed people I didn't have sex with, but I haven't had a guy in my bed I was actually interested in since Ben.

Connor said he wasn't good at the other stuff, but he wasn't giving himself enough credit, because right now I feel all-in on a guy I met just three days ago, and it's all his fault for being deliciously shy, until he's not.

"Hey." The man himself stands in my doorway. He's really more than cute—he's legit handsome, with dark scruff on his jaw, those thick brows, his perfect head of hair.

Ben wasn't particularly handsome, but he had a magnetism to him.

Connor attracts me in a different way. The way you want to reach out and touch a plush teddy bear. He's approachable. He's *nice*.

Ben wasn't nice, not deep down.

So why am I nervous? It's not like I'm afraid Connor's going to hurt me. We'd have to be a hell of a lot farther along than two pseudo-dates for that.

I guess it's normal to be nervous for firsts. The first time I opened the shop, I was shaking in my Chelsea boots, terrified I wouldn't remember how to work the point-of-sale app, or someone would try to shoplift, or I'd get an order for a bouquet of something I didn't have in stock.

But when the first customer came in and I managed to ring them up without setting the place on fire, I got over myself and things were fine.

I just need to move past the first-time jitters.

"Are you okay?" Connor's sitting next to me now, on my bed. "I can leave, if you want. I'm sure the roads are drivable."

"No, it's not that." I shift, canting my hip so I can look at him straight on. "It's been a while since I've had someone in my bed. I'm psyching myself out."

"Oh." He shifts, too, so we're both sitting with one leg tucked up underneath us, the other resting on the floor. "It's been a while for me, too."

"Yeah?"

"Yeah. My social circle sort of disintegrated after vet school. I started working a lot, and, like I said, I've never been good at the dating thing."

"Why not? You seem like the type of guy anyone would want to take home to the parents."

He shrugs as if he doesn't know the answer, but I can tell he's holding something back.

"What about you—Rosedale may be cooler now but there can't be a huge dating scene," he says.

"That was part of the appeal at first," I admit. "I was in a never-dating-again frame of mind when I decided on Rosedale."

"There's a story there."

"Yeah." Do I want to tell him about Ben? It's not a big

deal, but I honestly don't want to spend our time together rehashing all that old shit. "Maybe another time."

"Okay," he says easily. "So we're both a little rusty. And neither of us was expecting the night to go this way."

"But I'm glad it did," I say, because there's no point in not being honest.

"Me too. I love this quilt, by the way." He skims his fingers over the bed covering, a hand-stitched kaleidoscope of forget-me-not blue and mint green triangles.

Pleased, I stroke the soft fabric. "I got it from a local quilter at the farmers' market a couple of weeks after I moved here. It was a splurge, but I had to have it."

"It's cozy, and it matches your eyes. Sometimes they look blue, and sometimes they look green."

"They're blue, last I checked."

He reaches for my hand and picks it up carefully. "Can I ask about your tattoos?" He pushes my long-sleeved tee up my arm, revealing my forearm and its tapestry of colorful ink. I've got a peony flower, and a bee, a rainbow pride heart, a dandelion with half its seeds blowing away in an invisible wind. The tip of a feather peeks out under where my sleeve stops.

"Sure."

"When did you get your first one?"

I grin. "On my eighteenth birthday. I'd been saving all summer. My birthday is in September, so I cut out early from the first day of senior year to get it."

"Which one is it?" He traces the feather with a gentle forefinger, and I make a decision. If this light of a touch makes me shiver with want, I'd be an idiot to talk myself out of good sex with a handsome man.

So I take off my shirt—both of them, actually, since I have a thin thermal layer on underneath my henley. I don't have much body fat, and I get cold without my layers.

I toss the shirts to the side and look down, pointing to the starfish on my shoulder. "That was my first one."

Connor's not looking at the tattoo, though, when I raise my eyes to him. His gaze is glued to my chest, where twin silver bars decorate my nipples.

I unsuccessfully smother a smirk. "I got those when I turned twenty-one."

"Ah. They look good," he says, sounding strangled. His eyes finally find mine, their brown color almost black in the low light. "Fuck. Shay."

"You wanna touch?"

"Hell yes," he says fervently.

"Go slow, okay?" I've had guys attack them and come uncomfortably close to ripping them out.

"Of course," he murmurs. "Hang on." And then he whips off his own shirt, revealing developed pecs, his nipples small rust-colored buds standing to attention. I gulp audibly. He must work out, because his body is hard, his muscles defined.

"Fair's fair, right?" he says, sounding pleased with my reaction.

"Fair's fair," I echo, then I up the ante by unbuckling my belt and undoing my fly. My cock's been slowly filling since he started touching my arm, and I sigh when my erection is finally free from the confines of my corduroys. It's being held in place by my boxer briefs, but I don't want to get all the way naked yet, or this will all be over sooner than I'd like.

His gaze fixed on my chest, Connor mirrors my actions—getting the fly of his jeans open and putting his hand over the bulge in his underwear. His jeans hang off his hips low enough that I can tell he's wearing briefs, dark blue or black, and the sliver of his upper thigh I can see makes me want to rethink the whole not-getting-naked-yet idea.

"You look good," I say appreciatively.

"Yeah, um, you too," he says.

Then he's up in my space, kissing me hard, pressing me into the bed. He grinds our cocks together, and it's outrageously hot already. I lick into his mouth, loving the feeling of him on top of me. Then the blunt pads of his fingers graze my left nipple and a bolt of pleasure shoots from my chest to my cock and I arch up.

"Fuck, they're sensitive, huh?" he says, sounding dazed. His lips are swollen, and he brushes my other nipple, still lightly, as instructed, but with enough inten-tion that I curve up again. I touch myself there when I'm masturbating, but it's just not the same as when it's someone else's fingers.

"Yeah, Connor." I moan as he thumbs the bars back and forth, worrying them in a motion that has my cock full to bursting. He leans down and swipes his tongue over the buds of flesh, then blows on them, and I swear to all that is holy I almost come.

I think I mentioned that it's been a while.

I manage to hold on, literally gripping his meaty

shoulders with all my force, frantically rubbing up against him, but the bulky fabric gets in the way.

"Pants off," I beg, and we break apart long enough to shed our pants and socks, and then I dive under the covers, wanting protection from the chill of the air. I hold up the sheet and quilt for Connor to join me, his tight briefs sexier than they have any right to be.

The bed is small—only a double—and I'm tall and he's built, but we manage to fit. We go back to kissing, touching, and I remember what Connor said about being good at sex as he subtly leads the progression of things, his hands sure on my skin, firm and coaxing as he explores my body. Yes, he spends a lot of time on my piercings, but he pays attention to other parts of me, too. He kneads my ass with his strong hands, slotting me against him with delicious pressure. He kisses his way across my jaw and down my neck. I get my hands in his thick, gorgeous hair and tug, and at that he moans so loud it makes me glad I don't have neighbors. I tug again, and then he's got both of our cocks out of our underwear and is somehow stroking us off together. Whenever I try to do it, I can't work up any proper rhythm, but he's got the magic touch, and the slip and slide of his dick against mine feels so fucking good I'm coming before I realize it, pure pleasure washing through me for a blessedly long moment. He comes, too, right after, with his tongue in my mouth and a moan I can feel in my tonsils.

It's sexy hot for a moment as we come down, and then it's just squishy and wet and messy as I figure out most of it ended up on my belly.

"Tissues," I say, panting. If I move, I'm going to transfer our spend to the sheets. He grabs the box from the table and wipes us both as clean as he can, tossing the used tissues in the general direction of the wastebasket.

I pull up my underwear and collapse back against my pillows, then lift my head and fish one out for Connor to use. I wish I had more pillows, but I hadn't exactly shopped for two when I was furnishing the place.

"Wow." Connor turns to me and smiles lazily. "I needed that." He closes his eyes.

"Me too."

"Yeah?" He squints one eye open at me. "It felt really good to me."

"So far, all evidence points to yes, you are good at sex."

"Thank goodness," he says. "I was worried I wouldn't be able to cash that check."

"Consider it cashed. Though I wouldn't mind further demonstrations."

"Noted. You know, you don't play fair with these things," he says, touching my left piercing lightly.

"You think?" I like the way he touches them, reverently, but assertively. "Some guys I've been with don't know what to do with them. Hang on." I wasn't exactly taking inventory while we were rutting against each other, but now that we're settled in the bed, I see the telltale mark of black ink on Connor's hip. "You have a tattoo?"

He puts his hand over his eyes. "I do."

"Can I see?"

He hesitates for a second, then turns on his side and

pushes down the waist band of his briefs to expose a small line drawing tattoo of a rabbit.

"A bunny?" It wasn't what I was expecting, if I'd expected anything at all.

"It's a mini lop ear. I had one as a kid. Its name was Rabbit."

"Very descriptive."

"Shut up. I was four."

"Well, it's sweet," I say.

He grunts at the word. "I got it when I first moved to Chicago. I was trying to figure myself out. I thought maybe I was the kind of person who got tattoos."

I take a wild guess. "But you aren't?"

"Does that make me too boring to fuck?" he asks, semi-seriously.

I look at him, really look at him. I lean forward and kiss him, slowly and solemnly. "You're not boring. And we haven't fucked yet. But we will."

His smile is absurdly cute. "I like your tattoos, though." He traces my dandelion. "How come you only have one sleeve done?"

"I think I'm good with just one arm. I still have some room." I point to a few blank spots on my bicep. "I am the kind of person who gets tattoos, but I don't want my whole body covered or anything."

"I like those, too." His eyes drop to my piercings. "A lot."

"I could tell," I say dryly.

He tears his gaze away and looks at me sheepishly. "They're crazy hot. You're crazy hot."

"I'm glad you think so."

"Is it okay if I stay here tonight, really?" He suddenly looks unsure.

"It's okay with me. You need to let anyone know where you are?"

His entire body goes rigid. "Shit. I forgot about my parents." He sits up, narrowly missing hitting his head on the low ceiling, then leaps out of bed, diving for his jeans to pull out his phone.

I can't help chuckling at him. "Dude. You're—wait. How old are you?"

"Twenty-eight."

"You're twenty-eight," I repeat to prove my point.

"I know, I just—I'm staying there. I don't want them to worry." He fires off a text, thinks for a minute and writes a second one, then puts his phone on the side table. He seems tense, like a kid who's afraid his parents are going to ground him for missing curfew. I get not wanting them to worry, but he's not actually a kid.

He takes one last look at his phone, then turns to me. "Should I turn off the lamp?"

I lean over and blow out the candle. "Not yet. I'm going to brush my teeth. I might have an extra toothbrush."

"Sweet, thanks."

We cram together in the bathroom to brush our teeth, still in our underwear, smiling at each other's foamy mouths in the mirror. It's strangely one of the most inti-mate things we've done. When we get back to bed, we kiss for a while, our tongues minty fresh. Then we pull the covers up over our heads and shift around, trying to make the small bed work for us. In the end, I go little spoon, curled up on my side facing the wall. With Connor behind me, a solid, warm weight at my back, I fall into a deep winter's sleep.

make the small bed work for us. In the end, I go little spoon, curled up on my side facing the wall. With Connor behind me, a solid, warm weight at my back, I fall into a deep winter's sleep.

TWELVE

CONNOR

WHEN I WAKE UP, I have no idea where I am. Then I smell fresh grass and sandalwood, and I remember I'm with Shay. We're in his bed, a hand-made quilt keeping us warm and cozy. My nose feels cold where it pokes out above the covers, so I bury it in the first soft thing I encounter, which turns out to be Shay's fantastic hair, the soft, fine strands covering the base of his neck. I breathe in, his smell turning me on. Or maybe I'm turned on by the way my cock is nestled against the small of his back, the sensation of rubbing off on each other fresh in my mind. A precious memory, honestly.

I'd been so turned on I could barely see straight, and I'd had to struggle to live up to my self-imposed reputation as being "good at sex." I chuckle to myself at my bravado. Thank god Shay seems to like overconfident guys with pierced nipple obsessions.

I didn't know I had a piercing obsession until last night, but it turns out I do. When it's Shay's nipples that are pierced, anyway. The sight of those little metal bars went straight to my dick, and I'm definitely not over it. Just thinking about touching them again, about making Shay feel good by stroking them, has my cock swelling with morning wood harder than rebar.

Shay's probably still asleep, so I don't let myself give in to the desire to rut against him. I'm a guest, and I want to be invited back. Instead, I roll away, even though every instinct I have tells me to stay exactly where I am.

I poke my arm out of the covers and am able to reach my phone without moving too far out of my cocoon of warmth. I briefly check the time—it's later than I thought, much later than I've been getting up for work. It's so late it's given my parents time to text me.

Last night I'd texted them both that I was staying over at a friend's house because of the snow, following up with the note that I'd see them tomorrow.

My dad wrote back last night.

OK

Okay.
And this morning, my mom added:

Roads are clear now.

All right, this isn't a big deal. I am twenty-eight, as Shay helpfully pointed out last night. My parents are treating me like an adult. Good. That's good.

But I still feel slightly uneasy. What exactly am I going to tell them? I keep hoping if I drop enough clues they'll read between the lines, and I'll never actually have to say the words. It would all be so much easier if they just sort of got that I was not straight, and we could all proceed as if nothing had changed.

This sleepover situation is not one I ever expected to be in. Not being out at home was never a big deal, though it was occasionally annoying and sometimes uncomfortable.

But it's gone on this long because I've never had a crossing of the streams like this before. No date to explain away as something else. No overnight sleepover to blame on the snow.

My gut churns when I realize I'm either going to have to outright lie to my parents or do a masterful job of being vague and omitting certain details, which is basically the same thing.

I snuggle back up against Shay, my erection gone, and take comfort in being where I am right now, warm and safe, with all my problems wrapped in cellophane to save for another time.

Somehow, I manage to fall back asleep.

THE NEXT TIME I open my eyes, Shay is awake. He's facing me and our knees are bent toward each other, touching lightly. His eyes are heavy-lidded and his hand is propped up under his head.

"Hey." I'm less awake than my first rising, the heat trapped from our bodies under the covers keeping me lethargic and heavy.

"Hey," he says. "Sleep okay?"

"Yeah." I yawn, my brain trying to get itself more oxygen. "You?"

"Yeah." He smiles. "I had good dreams."

My stomach flips with excitement. He's so damn hot. "That's good," I whisper. My arousal grows. Neither of us wore shirts to sleep, and the bed smells ripe with our bodies. He curves toward me, hesitates. I close the distance, kissing him, heedless of morning breath. The sourness fades quickly as we lick into each other's mouths. Fuck. I could do this all day, pressed up against him in this perfect bubble where the outside world is just a theoretical imagining, and the only thing that's real is the two of us, making each other feel good.

I experimentally brush my hand against the front of his crotch, pleased to find him on his way to being fully hard. My cock responds in turn, and it's not long before the temperature rises even more. We shove down our underwear and his hands find my ass and pull me flush to him. Pressed together foot to head, the blankets smothering us lightly—I feel so fucking good I never want to leave this bed.

He releases my ass, bends his head down to swipe at my nipples with his tongue, and bites them lightly. I buck against him, then roll over to get the upper hand, pushing him against the mattress so I can get my mouth on his nipples. He hisses and grabs my hips as I get my fill of flesh, the tang of metal making me so hard it almost hurts.

I pull off and inspect him. His nipples are red and puffy and I'm afraid I've gone too far, except when I check in, Shay's eyes are glassy, and he's got a satisfied smile on his face. "Okay?"

"Hell yes," he says. His hands grip my waist, and now the blankets are at my back, and the light from the tiny window under the eve by the bed illuminates his long flat chest and belly, the faint trail that leads to his pubes, darker blond than his hair, which is spread over the pillow behind him in a silky wave. "I want you to come on them."

My cock pulses at the idea, and he reaches over with his long arm to grab lube out of a box by his bed. He hands it to me, and I waste no time slathering on the stuff. He watches me do it, and I realize his cock's trapped behind me, rubbing against my crack, but he doesn't have the leverage to do anything with it. I climb off him, shuffle forward on my knees, so I'm kneeling next to his chest.

I hand him back the lube. "Jerk off with me?" I suggest, and he nods, lubing himself up before tossing the bottle to the side. He bites his lip, still watching me stroke myself, so I make it a bit of a show, letting the head suggestively peek out of the ring of my fingers. I speed up my hand and he speeds up his. I lean down and kiss him once, hard. "You want me to shoot on your chest?"

"Yeah," he says, breathless. "Do it. Come on."

I slow down, wringing all the pleasure I can out of every stroke. He groans in frustration. "Come on, Connor, I wanna see it."

"You wanna see me come on your beautiful nipples?" I reach out and touch one lightly. He hisses, nods frantically.

"So hot." I increase my pace, no longer holding back.

I want it to last longer, but I can't deny that I need to see my come painting his chest as much as he wants to see me do it. His gaze is fixed on my cock—he never looks away, not even when I start shooting. I aim for his nips, the thick milky stuff decorating him like he was born to wear come.

My come.

Once I'm wrung out and drop my hand from my oversensitive cock, Shay closes his eyes, bites his lip and really goes at it. I glance at his long rosy pink cock in his long-fingered hand and wish I could get hard again already. Instead, I push some of my come over his nipples, rub it in lightly.

"Oh, fuck." That's the warning I get before Shay's coming, his own release coating his fingers and making a mess of his pubes. It seems like he comes for a long time, during which I memorize how hot he looks with his eyes screwed shut in pleasure, his chest marked up, his cock pulsing in his hands.

Slowly, he opens his eyes. I think I'm grinning at him, because I don't seem to have much control over my facial movements at the moment, and I feel light and buoyant, as if nothing can bring me down. He grins back, then says, "Well. Good morning."

I laugh. I can't help it. I just feel so...good. "Good morning."

He glances down at his body. I track his gaze, what he sees. A fucked-out, super-hot, naked man covered in jizz.

"I'm a mess." He doesn't sound mad about it.

"You look incredible." I know it's only our second

time, but damn. "I think you look good wearing my come."

He gives me a wicked smile. "Me too."

"Shay." I kiss him because I can't not. I only stop when a dull buzzing sound breaks through the ocean of endorphins I'm swimming in.

"Uh. Is that your phone?" Shay props himself up on his elbows, looks in the direction of the buzzing.

I stare at the device, honestly not understanding that I'm supposed to answer it, if only to make the buzzing stop. Having sex with Shay has melted my brains out of my ears, apparently.

"Right." I grab it up, and it silences. The missed call notification pops up on screen. My mom. I'm about to call her back when the text pops up.

> Emergency patient. If I don't hear from you, I'll leave for the office in three minutes.

"Shit." I hit the call button as fast as I can, and Mom picks up on the first ring.

"Sorry, missed the call. Who's the patient?"

"The Gunderson cat swallowed some sort of medication and is showing signs of toxicity. It might need a transfusion, in which case you have to call the animal hospital in Danbury. Can you handle it?"

"Absolutely. I'm on it."

"How far out are you?" Mom asks. Fair question.

I run a hand through my hair and hedge. "I'm close. Give me fifteen minutes."

"I'll tell them to meet you at the office. Thanks."

"Sorry I—" I want to apologize for not being quicker to pick up her call, but she's already hung up, probably to call the Gundersons. Shit. My heart's racing again, and it's not because of Shay. Well, it is because of Shay, because if I hadn't been wrapped up with him in bed, I would have been home, and my mom wouldn't have had to possibly risk her recovery to do the job I'm supposed to do.

"What's wrong?" Shay asks, full of concern as I slide out of bed.

"I have to go. Emergency at the office."

"No problem. What can I do?"

"Um. Do you have any black tea? Maybe a bagel or something?"

"On it." He's already scooting off the end of the bed. He's so tall he has to duck to put on his clothes, not bothering to clean up first.

I force myself to get dressed without thinking too hard about the fact that he's still got my come on his skin, then use the bathroom to freshen up. By the time I come out and get my boots on, Shay hands me a travel mug of tea and a piece of toast slathered in almond butter.

"You're a lifesaver. I hate to run out on you."

"Hey, I get it. You're the one who's a lifesaver. Can you go out the back? The back door opens without a key, but if you want to go out the front, I have to let you into the shop."

"The back is fine." I leave before I do something stupid, like give him a proper kiss that will delay me even further.

I run down the stairs, exit out the back of the building. For a second, I'm confused as to why I don't see Mom's SUV parked in the shallow lot, until I remember I parked on Linden Street before game night. I let myself into the office and turn on the lights. I wash my hands again, replace my clothes with fresh scrubs, bump up the heat, and am ready when there's a knock at the door.

Time to do my job.

THIRTEEN
SHAY

THE REST of the morning feels pretty anticlimactic after having hot sex with Connor, then having him run out before the afterglow even wore off. I putter around feeling sorry for myself that our unexpected night together ended so abruptly but then shake myself out of it. He's got obligations, and so do I. Besides, we have a date for the fundraiser tonight.

I debate making myself coffee versus going to Hot Brew. When I look out the window, there's a crust of snow on everything, but we didn't get more than an inch total. Linden Street hasn't even been plowed; it's simply been cleared by cars driving on it. The sight of the barely there snow makes me smile. Connor didn't exactly need to stay over, but he clearly wanted to.

I flutter a little, remembering how confident he was, how he kept checking in with me. I think confident-but-not-aggressive-in-bed is my new type.

Connor's my new type, period.

I scratch my belly, remember why it's itchy. Okay,

shower, Hot Brew, then I face the rest of the day. And maybe it's sappy, but if I happen to sing in the shower, who's to know but me?

MEADOW USUALLY HAS SUNDAYS OFF, so I'm confused to find her at Hot Brew when I tumble in close to noon.

"Hey you," I say, pleased to see her, my heart full of enthusiasm for all the glorious people of the world. "Didn't expect to see you here."

She looks at me suspiciously. "Someone called out. You're a ray of sunshine this m—oh," she answers her unvoiced question, nodding sagely. "You and Connor did it."

I shush her, but no one's within earshot, or if they are, they aren't paying any attention to us. I lean in and whisper, "He spent the night."

"Well, good. He was a good guy in high school. A little square, but not a jerk. I'm happy for you."

"Thanks."

"The usual?"

"Sure. Did you and Melissa have a good night?"

"Oh, yeah." She smiles for real at the question. "We did some prom role-playing. You know, the closeted prom queen and the girl she wants to experiment with? It was pretty steamy."

I laugh. "TMI, but good for you." Something about her description of their fantasy snags on the back of my mind, but I can't quite pinpoint what it is. Meadow goes to make my coffee, and I mentally shrug, then check the flower shop's social media feeds, cheerfully responding to a DM asking our hours, even though they're clearly listed in the bio.

"See you later at the thing?" I ask when Meadow returns a few minutes later with my lidless flat white.

"See you there."

I spend the afternoon assembling the flower arrangement for the event, and a smaller basket of goodies that I'm—well, technically the shop is—donating to the silent auction, pleased with the result.

If I owned this place the responsibility would be all mine, but so would the satisfaction. I managed to get a meeting set up with someone at the bank tomorrow, since the shop is closed on Mondays as well. Fingers crossed for a miracle.

I save time to primp before Connor's due to pick me up. I haven't heard from him all day, but I figure he's busy with his pet emergency. I hope everyone's all right. I can't imagine the stress of being a vet, working to save animals people love, sometimes not being able to.

Shit. I'm falling for this guy, I think to myself as I bend over the sink in the bathroom and brush my hair. My initial attraction to him has only increased, and I'm fully crushing on him now. Obviously, the sex moved things along, but what else am I supposed to do but melt when faced with a nice, hot guy who knows exactly what to do with my body?

I'm ready to go, hair as good as it's going to get, the barest dab of cologne on my wrists, looking good, if I do say so myself, in dark jeans, a hunter green loose peasant-style shirt topped with a brown vest, my Chelsea boots, a fancy belt with a big western-style silver buckle, and my usual assortment of bracelets and rings. I wait in the shop, since that's where the basket and the flower arrangement are, but now it's after five and there's no text from Connor to let me know he's here.

I send him a text at ten past.

> Hey, hope everything's okay. I have to get the flowers to the Art Center. Meet me there?

I wait for the typing bubble or a read receipt but there's nothing, so I push aside my worry and double check the shop is locked before heading to the back parking area. I load the heavy arrangement and basket into the back of the van, shivering in the cold night air. Though most of the snow melted during the day, there's still some gathered on the windshield, so I have to scrape it off and get the front of my jacket all wet in the process. I'm in a thoroughly crappy mood by the time I get to the Art Center, late, wet, and stung by the lack of communication from Connor. Is it wrong of me to hope something's wrong and that he's not standing me up?

"There you are," Jack says when I arrive at the front, juggling my offerings awkwardly. He takes the basket. "People are starting to arrive."

"Great." I grunt in frustration. "Where do you want this?" I hoist the big arrangement, which is meant to be a decoration.

"Let me ask Pete. Is everything okay? I thought Connor was supposed to come."

"Yeah, me too," I say sourly. "He didn't show."

"Oh, damn." Jack gives me a sympathetic glance that makes me even grumpier. Only thing worse than being stood up is people feeling sorry for you for being stood up.

"Whatever," I say. "Can you find out where this is supposed to go?"

Jack disappears and I wait in the entryway, the arrangement feeling heavier with each passing second. I'm about to set it on the floor and go find Jack when I hear the thin ring of my phone in my back pocket.

My pulse jumps. I quickly bend over to set the decoration down so I can answer the call, but the vase slips, and I lose my grip. The heavy glass thunks on the hard tile floor. To my surprise, it doesn't break, but it does slosh over, half the stems dislodging, water splashing everywhere. "Damn."

I right the vase, and Jack walks up just as I pull my phone out to see the missed call—from my brother.

"What happened? Pete wants this by the bar."

"Nothing," I say, suddenly super tired. "I'll fix this. Can you grab a towel or something?"

"Sure."

Jack cleans up the water and I find the bar, which has been set up in the main gallery. Within a few minutes, the arrangement looks almost as good as when I first put it together.

"You have a gift," Pete says, walking up to me with a smile. He's about my height, so we can look directly into each other's eyes.

"I try." A steady stream of people enters the room,

heading for the food and checking out the walls, which feature new pieces of art created by the Art Center's students. A bluegrass trio plays in the corner. Ariana, from the wine shop in town, is bartending and I catch her eye. "Can I get a glass of red?" I turn to Pete. "Wait, this shindig is open bar, right?"

"Yep," Pete says cheerfully. "Drunk people tend to donate more."

"Devious."

"Hey, are you okay?"

I take a gulp of wine and regret it when I start coughing. "I'm fine." I finger my phone in my pocket, wonder if Connor's texted me.

"Okay, well, have fun," he says, not sounding convinced. I wave him off—this is a busy night for him, having to make the rounds and glad-hand donors—then give in to the urge to look at my phone.

I only see the missed call from Tye. I text him back.

> Call you later? At an event.

> Oh right, your date. Have fun

Tye's cheerful reply only make me feel worse. I thumb over to the last message I sent Connor. Is it pathetic to contact him again?

If I'm actually being stood up, then yes.

But if something prevented him from making our date, then I'd be the asshole not to reach out.

I quickly type out the message and hit send.

> Is everything okay? Let me know when you can.

I don't mention I'll be at the fundraiser for another couple of hours at least, because I don't want to spend the whole night hoping he'll walk through the doors only to be disappointed. I've been through that enough times to know it's a waste of energy. Instead, I resolve not to look at my phone for the rest of the night. I put it on silent, finish my wine, and go to scope out the auction items. I don't really have cash to spare at the moment, but it can't hurt to bid up a few things, can it?

WHEN I FINALLY STUMBLE OUT OF the office's back entrance, careful to activate the security system and lock the door even in my daze, it's full-on dark and very cold. I've been inside all day, aside from when I met each of my three back-to-back emergency patients at the front to let them in. I've been running on energy bars and tea since I left Shay's, and I'm exhausted. I trudge around to Linden where I left mom's car twenty-four hours ago. There's still snow on the windshield, and I hope she's got a scraper in the trunk. Glancing at the dark windows of the flower shop, I suddenly remember and feel sick.

It's Sunday. The day of the fundraiser at the Rosedale Art Center. We confirmed last night. I was supposed to pick him up over an hour ago. And I forgot.

I grapple for my phone in my coat pocket. I have a few missed texts—one from Courtney, one from my mom reminding me to set the alarm when I leave, and two from Shay.

I know it's hard to convey tone in texts, but Shay's

comes through loud and clear. He sounds worried-slash-pissed, and I don't blame him. I stood him up after our amazing night together. He should be pissed.

Only what do I do now? I'm grimy after my unexpectedly full day of work, rumpled, and probably smell of five different unpleasant things. That's something I didn't realize until I started interning—being a vet means you get up close and personal with a lot of bad smells. I barely notice them at this point, but I know I'm in no shape to mingle at a party. I'm also starving and my head hurts from the tense day. But I can't just leave Shay hanging.

I know where the Rosedale Art Center is, but I don't trust myself to navigate in the dark when I'm this tired, so I put the address into my phone. I'm not exactly sure what I'm going to do when I get there, but I have to do something. I blast the heat, trying to warm up, and I get there five minutes later. The parking lot is pretty full, but I find a spot. The florist van parked off to the side means Shay's got to be here.

I smooth my hair, grimace at my image in the rearview mirror. I have serious five o'clock shadow and purple smudges under my eyes. But when I think about trying to explain via text, my stomach churns. Better to do this in person.

The Art Center is a midcentury modern building on a beautiful plot of land at the top of a hill. I vaguely remember taking a drawing class here one summer as a kid, and not being particularly good at it, but liking the quirky instructor. The lobby is warmly lit and has small sculptures set into recesses and vibrant paintings on the walls. I'm greeted by someone with a shaved head wearing a pantsuit and big dangly earrings.

"Can I help you?"

"I'm looking for Shay Brierley."

The person points me inside. "I last saw him at the silent auction, in the green room. Don't forget to bid."

I thank them and make my way in. I'm grateful not to run into anyone I know—Meadow or Jack or any of the people who probably think I'm a total jerk for standing Shay up.

I spend a minute looking in vain for a green room before I spot a sign for the Greene Room. Okay. I duck inside. Long tables are set up with all sorts of baskets and displays advertising different items. And Shay's there, in front of a basket of goodies that must have come from the flower shop. His back is to me, so I can see what he's wearing—ass-hugging jeans, a loose shirt, and a vest. His hair is brushed smooth, and he looks long and lean and delicious.

And he's talking to a guy.

The guy is facing me, and I eye him critically. He's shorter than Shay but taller than me, and he's got curls, buttery yellow like you might see in a Renaissance painting. His mouth is lush, his complexion peaches and cream. He's wearing black slacks and a thin white Oxford shirt that's unbuttoned to his sternum. I hate him on sight. He laughs at something Shay says, and my venom increases exponentially.

I thread my way through the tables and tap Shay on the arm. He turns to me, surprise in his eyes.

"Oh my god, Connor, are you okay?" He sounds

more relieved to see me than mad. I'm such a jerk for making him worry.

"I can't believe I missed our date." I'm not even shy about using the word in my desire to underline the situation to the handsome blond guy, who I purposefully ignore. "I can explain—emergency patients, yada yada, but I feel terrible about it."

"Hey, it's fine," he says gently. "Uh, Connor, this is Toby. Toby, this is Connor Nieves, he's—"

"The new vet. I've heard about him. Ivy and I are patients of your mother—well, not us, but our cat." Toby has a light British accent and a friendly demeanor.

I offer a bland smile. "Ivy?"

"My girlfriend," he says.

"Oh. Well, that's great," I say, ten pounds of relief sliding off my shoulders. "Nice to meet you," I add belatedly.

"Same. Well, I better add my number to a few more of these lots," Toby says. "See you later, Shay."

"See you," Shay says, sounding slightly amused. Toby wanders off, and I feel silly about my knee-jerk jealous reaction. "So, no offense, Connor, but you kind of look like hell."

"I came straight from work." Shay looks all put together, and he smells incredible—that mix of sandalwood and fresh soil. I feel like a piece of gum someone chewed and spit out on the sidewalk. "You look fantastic."

"Thanks," he says. "But you didn't have to come all the way out here. You must be exhausted."

"I am. I just—I didn't want you to think I forgot.

Which, to be completely honest, I did. But it was because we had the cat toxicity case, and then there was a dog who'd been in a fight and needed sutures, and then, finally, a sick rat."

"It's okay," Shay says. "Really. I'm just glad you're okay. But you should go home and get some rest. Don't you have to work again in the morning?"

"Well, yeah. But what about our date?"

"We'll have to do it another time."

"Another time," I repeat, getting a sinking sensation that I'm getting the brush-off. Which maybe I deserve, but still. Last night meant a lot to me, but what if it didn't mean anything to Shay? What if he's interested in this Toby guy? Girlfriend aside, Toby certainly looked like he was enjoying the one-on-one time with my—with Shay.

Shay could have anyone he wants.

I glare at the attractive Brit where he's scribbling his name on a silent auction sheet two rows away.

"What's going on?" Shay asks, lowering his voice. "You aren't—you aren't jealous of Toby, are you?" His tone is hard to read—incredulity mixed with something else. Fondness?

"No, of course not." I immediately deny it, scrub a hand over my face. "I'm really beat. I shouldn't have even come here."

"Hey." He reaches out and touches my arm lightly. The first time he's touched me since I arrived. "I'm glad you came. It was sweet. And we'll talk tomorrow. But now you should go home and rest."

It feels less like a brush-off now and more like he

actually cares about me. And since my head is swimming with exhaustion and hunger, I agree.

"I'm going to do that. But I'll make this up to you," I promise. That's the least I can do. And besides, I'm already counting the time until I can see him again.

His answering smile gives me strength to walk back to my car and get home in one piece. I manage to shower before throwing myself into bed without bothering to eat. I'm out before I can count to ten.

FIFTEEN

SHAY

I HAVE an appointment at the bank Monday morning, so I hoist myself up and out of bed on the early side. I even avoid bonking my head on the ceiling. I make my own coffee in a fit of fiscal responsibility, eat breakfast, and check my email. I remember I never called my brother back, but I'll have to do that after the bank meeting.

The Rosedale Bank and Trust is downtown near the library, within walking distance. It's another cold morning, but the snow is all gone, so it's an easy walk bundled up in my warmest jacket, gloves, scarf, and hat. I've brought my computer in a satchel in case I need it.

I walk into the warm seventies-era lobby, then quickly get seated in a blue chair across from Daryl, a forty-something guy with wire-rimmed glasses. Daryl is sympathetic, but upfront about my chances of qualifying for a loan the size I'd need to buy the building with my lack of assets. It turns out getting a loan is hard when you don't have much collateral, or a steady income. On paper,

I don't make much from the business that I've poured my heart and soul into for a year and a half.

Still, Daryl says his bank has a special interest in investing in local businesses, so if I assemble what seems like fifty different types of paperwork, from my tax returns and pay stubs to a business plan, he'll run the numbers and see what he can do.

I leave feeling pretty low about my prospects, with what feels like homework, thanks to the documents I'll need to find. But I'll see this through because otherwise my only other option to make this happen is to do something I really don't want to do.

Ask my parents for the money.

I call Tye after lunch. "How's Jen?"

"She's better. We talked, and it really helped, thanks."

"That's great." At least someone's life is going right.

"How did your date go with the vet tech?"

"He's not a vet tech. He's just a vet."

"And how did it go?" he asks in an impatient big brother's voice.

I consider lying, but that would make last night seem worse than it actually was. "Well, he kind of accidentally missed our date last night, but he said he'd make it up to me."

There's a pause. "Shay." The single word holds an entire paragraph's worth of judgement.

"It's not like that," I protest. "He had a work emergency. And he was very apologetic."

"Okay. Sure." Tye sounds unconvinced.

"It's not like Ben."

"Good."

"Seriously—it's totally too soon to say that I really like him, but I really like him." I do. The amount of relief I felt when he showed last night indicates just how much I was trying to convince myself I didn't care that he'd stood me up. And the way he got transparently jealous over me talking to Toby Wheaton—an objectively attractive human, but one who's in a serious relationship—was ego-bolsteringly adorable.

"I'm glad you like him; he just better deserve you. Sounds like you should take it slow."

I stay silent. I better not tell him we already slept together.

"Shay." How can he make one word sound so accusatory?

"Slow. Of course."

"You slept with him, didn't you?"

"Look, just because you and Jen waited for, like, months—"

"It was three weeks."

"Whatever. Connor is really, truly a nice guy. I promise. He's an animal doctor, for god's sake. And he gets along with my friends. And he's really sweet." I've clearly got to change the subject before my brother stages an intervention. "By the way, remember how the owner of Rosedale Flowers and More wants to sell the building?"

"Yeah, what's the status on that?"

"Well, I just came from the bank and I'm going to get them a bunch of paperwork but getting a loan might not be in the cards given my income."

"Oh, that sucks. You really want to do this, huh?"

"It's not exactly how I pictured owning my own business, but it's pretty exciting, yeah. But I don't think the money is just going to materialize."

"You could ask Mom and Dad, Shady."

"I want to do this on my own," I say. "No offense."

"None taken. But think about it. All businesses need capital to succeed. You have to get it from somewhere. I got it from Mom and Dad, and I don't regret it. It doesn't make your business less legitimate, or less yours."

"But would they even go for it? It's not exactly their style."

"But it is yours. And they love you. And they want you to succeed." He sighs. "It's only money. It doesn't have to mean everything."

I laugh. "True. Thanks for the pep talk."

"Anytime. I better go, work meeting in five at the new location."

"Love you, Tye Dye."

"Love you, bro."

CONNOR CALLS while I'm finishing up some orders to make sure I have enough stock on hand for the upcoming Valentine's Day rush. I know what was popular last year, which makes it way easier to plan for this year.

"Hey," he says, his voice scratchy.

"Are you okay?"

"Just tired. It's been another busy day. It's annoying

to call you when I'm right next door, but I don't have time to come over."

"It's okay." I'm worried about him, though. He seems to be overextended, taking on the entire vet practice on his own while his mom is out of commission. How does she do it all by herself?

"So about our date."

"I told you—it's fine."

"No, I mean our next date," he says. "I promised to make it up to you and I will. So I was wondering what kind of food do you like? Sushi? Italian? Tibetan?"

My stomach rumbles. "Oh. I like all kinds of things. I'm not picky."

"Give me something to go on. Your top three?"

"Hmmm." He's vegetarian, so I'm not about to request barbecue. "I guess I like the usual—pizza, like really good pizza, though. I can always go for Italian. Oh, and I love tamales, but you can't get good ones here, not that I've found, anyway."

"Okay, good to know. How's Friday night? I'd say we should try to do something sooner, but with work, I don't want to make plans and have to break them."

It's disappointing, but also considerate. "No, I get it. Friday's great."

"Cool. So I'll text you with particulars later."

"All right." We fall silent, but it's not awkward.

He breaks the silence first to say, "You looked really good last night, by the way."

I bite my lower lip to contain my smile. "You told me."

"I did? I was really out of it."

"I'm glad you got some rest. Sounds like you could use some more."

"Yeah. I'm fine. I wish I could have gone home with you."

"Two nights in a row?" I tease. "Sounds pretty serious." It's a joke, sort of. Tye's warning echoes in my head. Maybe I should be going slower, but maybe it's better to know now if Connor's not in this with me.

But he only says, "Yeah." His voice is lower than usual, and he doesn't sound like he's joking. My stomach flips.

"So Friday," I say, because I can't exactly invite him over to get in my bed right now, even if I'd totally be up for it.

"Friday. I'll text you."

"Looking forward to it."

"Me too, Sh—ah, me too." I hear someone murmuring in the background. "I gotta go," he says, briskly now.

"Okay, bye," I say right as the beeps indicating he's ended the call sound in my ear. It's an abrupt end to what was an encouraging conversation, but I remind myself he's got a demanding job, and I go back to work myself, promises of Friday echoing in my head.

"CHECK in with Violet at the front and she'll get you set up with a follow-up appointment," I say to Maggie Wainwright, then I scratch Sophie, her Australian Shepherd, under the chin. Sophie wags her tail appreciatively.

"Thank you so much, Dr. Nieves," Maggie says. "You've really set my mind at ease."

"Of course," I answer, opening the exam room door for owner and pet. My mother is standing on the other side of the door, holding her jacket over her broken arm. "Mom, what are you doing here?"

"This is my veterinary practice, last time I checked," she says, her eyes moving past me to the patient. "Hi Maggie, Sophie. How is everything?" She holds out the hand from her uninjured arm for Sophie to sniff.

"Your son is a treasure, Iris," Maggie says, her wrinkled apple-doll face creasing into a broad smile. "He's been so patient with Sophie."

"Good to hear," Mom says. "Connor, do you have a minute?"

"Of course. Four weeks until that follow-up," I remind Maggie, who waves at both of us as she heads for the front of the office. "What's up, Mom?" I can't help the rustle of nerves—that gut-churning feeling of being called into the principal's office, not sure what I did wrong.

But her answer is benign. "Oh, mostly I was sick of being cooped up at home. Your dad drove me down. He's doing some shopping. I'm meeting him at the bookstore in a while."

I walk with her to the break room, grab my thermos of tea, and refill my mug of the day—it says "everything tastes better with dog hair in it" in cartoon letters on the side.

"Do you want something to drink? I think there are some smoothies in the fridge." I've started stocking plenty of snacks and drinks in the office, since it's basically impossible to get away during the day. I'd have thought with Shay right next door I'd be able to sneak out to say hi once in a while, but back-to-back appointments keep me on my feet and away from my crush, which is probably for the best since I can't screw things up if I don't see him.

But I've been thinking about him an awful lot, especially about the way he looked Sunday morning, with my come on his chest, and Sunday night, all prettied up for that event. I've mostly gotten over the embarrassment of being that guy who messes up a date so badly—and instead, have been giving plenty of thought to Friday night, and where to take Shay that will be a home run.

"...you finding everything?" Mom's talking, and I realize I missed part of what she said. I put thoughts of Shay away and focus on my mom-slash-boss's words. "It's been a week, so now you have a feel for the place. You have everything you need? I know we're not as sophisticated as that big animal hospital you've been working at."

I'm quick to reassure her, not used to her sounding insecure. "No, it's been great. I've had to refer a couple of patients out to the bigger hospitals for surgery, but I like that we focus on general care here. I remember a lot of these families from when I was a kid. You've got a real community of patients."

She falters, as if she's not sure how to respond to the praise. "Oh. Well. That's good. I was afraid you'd think we didn't have the latest and greatest tech."

Mom, afraid of something? "No, your equipment is in good shape, and the techs know their stuff. Violet's on top of everything, as always. You have a good team."

She visibly relaxes. "Thanks. It's been so long since I had another vet in this office, I wasn't sure if maybe I'd gotten too set in my ways."

"I like your ways," I say with a smile. "Though I was thinking that some of your ordering could be streamlined. We used this software that made reordering really easy at the last place I worked. I'll get Violet the info and she can check it out if that's okay."

"That would be fine. Well, I'm sure you have more patients to see," she says, suddenly brusque.

"Always. I don't know how you've been handling this workload all by yourself, Mom."

"Well, I finally had to stop accepting new patients about six months ago. Violet was sick of me overbooking."

"Oh, I didn't know that." But it makes sense. I'm a

little surprised that Rosedale has so much business, but then again, I'm not. A lot of mom's patients are from surrounding communities because she's got such a stellar reputation.

"I better get going," she says, moving toward the door. "I don't want you to get behind."

"Well, it's good to see you, Mom." It's true—I've enjoyed stepping in and having the freedom to do my own thing, but I always thought if I was in this position, we'd be working together. Being a solo vet is a bit lonely. "Come back anytime."

"Oh, I will," she says sharply, reminding me yet again that this is her practice. Then she smiles with a hint of self-deprecation. "I know you all think I'm a workaholic, but I can't help loving my job. I miss the animals," she adds, seeming a bit self-conscious.

I smile. My mom's not perfect, but she definitely chose the right profession. "Why don't you go out the front and say hi to whoever's in the waiting room—I'm sure they'll be glad to see you."

"Okay, I'll do that," she says. We exchange a look, and I feel close to her in that single moment. And suddenly, I want that feeling all the time. I want her to let me in. I want her to know me.

I'm tired of being only part of myself around her.

But now's not the time for opening up. I've got patients waiting. Which is a convenient excuse to keep up the status quo.

Sometime, sooner rather than later, I need to find the strength to show her the rest of me.

We walk out to the front together.

Mom doesn't hug me on her way through the door to the waiting room, but she does pause and say, "If I had another full-time vet on staff, we could open up to new patients again. Think about it."

And then she leaves before I can respond.

THE WEEK PASSES QUICKLY, between the shop being steadily busy and my usual standing orders. I also have a birthday party and a retirement party to do arrangements for that I have to fit in between helping customers. My mom calls on Wednesday morning, and I think about how I didn't even know Connor existed when I spoke to her last Wednesday, and now we've not only slept together, but it feels like this could be the start of something serious.

I can't keep my good mood out of my voice, and she picks up on it immediately.

"What's new, Blueberry?"

"Well..." I consider telling her about Rodney and the building sale. Tye's advice echoes in my head. But something holds me back. "I met someone interesting." I give her the CliffsNotes version of meeting Connor, the fact that he's a vet and works next door, and that we're going out again on Friday.

"A doctor? That's so exciting."

"Yeah, he has like so much more schooling than me. Is that bad?" I mean, I went to college, but I've always been a more hands-on person than an academic brain.

"Well, you're business-savvy," she says reassuringly. "How is business?"

"Going into our busy time. Valentine's Day preorders are up over last year, and I have four weddings in February." I scribble a note to remind myself to lock down my wedding helpers' schedules.

"Dad and I were looking at flights," she says. "It seems like the best thing to do is fly to New York and rent a car."

"Hmmm?" I'm only half paying attention to my mom as a woman with a cast on her arm comes in and starts looking around. There's something familiar about her, and when Mom says something about a bed-and-breakfast, I hastily tell her I have to go and hang up.

"Can I help you?" I ask.

"Just browsing," she says, not looking my way.

I let her do her thing while I add more items to my to-do list for the week. She approaches the counter after a few minutes and says, "I'm Iris Nieves. You're doing the flowers for my daughter Courtney's wedding in a few weeks."

"That's right," I affirm, biting my tongue against an instant rush of nerves. This is Connor's mom. I'm usually pretty good with the parents, but there's something intimidating about Iris Nieves.

"My veterinary office is next door," she says.

Now I remember seeing her around town a couple of times. "I know. I mean—everyone says you're an amazing vet," I say, refraining from an instant wince. Was that laying it on too thick? "I'm not a pet owner, myself. Though I love animals. I know your son."

"Oh?" She looks confused. "Did you go to Rosedale High?"

"No, I'm from Arizona," I say, in a bit of a non sequitur. Why am I so flustered? "But he and I met the other day."

She gives me a distant polite smile; it's clear Connor hasn't mentioned me.

"Everything's set for the wedding. Just waiting on those centerpiece numbers," I add, in case she thinks I'm not up to the job.

"Twelve," she replies crisply.

"Great. I'll make a note of it."

After she leaves, I berate myself for being awkward. I didn't even tell her my name. I console myself with the fact that she clearly wasn't coming in to check out her son's potential boyfriend. The word makes my cheeks flame hot with possibility. But it seems that even though I've been talking Connor up to my mom and brother, Connor hasn't been doing the same. It's dispiriting, but then I give myself a pep talk. It's still early days in our relationship, not necessarily a red flag. I'm not giving up on him so soon.

FRIDAY AT WORK is blessedly light, and I'm able to head home to shower and change before I pick up Shay for our date.

I dress with care from the limited assortment of clothes I brought with me from Chicago, ending up with jeans, green thermal under a green checked shirt, boots, peacoat, scarf, and hat. I stick my toothbrush in an inner jacket pocket—what can I say? I'm an optimist. It's been clear since last weekend's snowfall, and it's supposed to continue to be cold with no snow in sight.

"I'm heading out." I poke my head into the kitchen, where my dad's puttering around. "I'll be back late." I think about how if our date ends in Shay's bed, I'm not going to want to leave, especially since I don't have to work tomorrow. My mother has a pre-existing arrangement with another vet in the area to be on-call on Saturdays. "Actually, I might stay over if I need to. So don't worry if I'm not here." I duck out again, hoping that covers my bases, but my dad's voice stops me.

"Connor Nieves—what do you mean you might stay over?"

"Just, you know, if it gets late," I call vaguely.

My dad comes out of the kitchen. "If what gets late?"

"Poker night," I say impulsively. "If I'm drinking and stuff, it'll be better just to crash."

My stomach churns at the lie. It's the first time I've outright lied since I got here, and it makes me feel sick. If I said I had a date, it might shut my dad up about my reasons for spending the night—my parents do not like talking about sex—but then he might ask who the date is with, and I'd have to make something up, which feels like it would be worse than the poker night thing.

He doesn't pick up on my internal turmoil. "Make smart choices," he tells me.

I don't remind him that I'm twenty-eight and have been living on my own for a decade, because I think what he's trying to say is he loves me. "Thanks, Dad."

Shay's waiting outside the flower shop when I pull up to the curb at 6:30 on the dot. I'm determined to win his trust back—admittedly, lying to my dad about where I'm going to be tonight isn't a great start.

But I push that aside to admire Shay. He's got his hair back, and his lips look kind of shiny, as if he's wearing a little gloss. He's got a big dramatic coat on, and he looks, well... incredible. Every time I see him, I fall for him more.

He slips into the passenger seat of my mom's SUV with grace, belying his height and gives me a smile.

"Damn, you look great," I say, then lean in and smell him. "You smell good, too. What is that?" I stay away from scented products because the animals in my care would rather smell my own natural scent than artificial ones. But that doesn't mean I don't enjoy it on Shay.

"Just a drop of cologne," he says. "Glad you aren't allergic."

"I think I'm the opposite of allergic. I want to take you right back upstairs."

He bites his shiny lip as if he's considering the idea.

"But I won't," I say heroically, "because we have dinner plans."

"You've been very mysterious about these plans," he says, buckling in.

Before I pull away from the curb, I have to ask, "Can I kiss you really quick? Your lips are driving me crazy."

He waves his hand in open invitation. "Take your time."

I tease him back by kissing him lightning fast, but I can't deprive myself for the sake of being funny, and I go back for a longer, more lingering kiss. His lips feel amazing underneath mine, soft and warm, and my hand finds his jaw without my realizing I've reached up to touch him. His skin is smooth, freshly shaven. At the idea of him shaving for me, I can't help a shiver. I haven't seen him in almost a week and the time apart has done nothing to dull my attraction to him.

The kiss goes on, and the cabin of the car suddenly feels overly warm. I reluctantly pull away to turn the heat down but find it's barely blowing. He just makes me hot. Or maybe we're generating the heat together. "Damn, Shay." I lick my lips, and he watches me with hooded eyes. "Um—"

"No," he says, voice low. "Dinner. You can ravish me later."

"Fair deal." I owe it to him to agree. I loosen my scarf and adjust my jeans briefly. When I glance over, Shay's smirking at my crotch. "What?" I say defensively. "I missed you." Shit. "I mean—"

"It's okay. I missed you, too."

"Okay." I smile to myself, pull the address of the restaurant up on my phone, and let the wonderful feeling of being missed settle into my bones.

On the drive to the restaurant, which is in a town about thirty minutes away, we talk about our weeks. I tell him about the interesting puppy birth I assisted in, and he tells me about the preparations he's been making for Valentine's Day, which is apparently the Super Bowl for florists. I wonder if giving a florist flowers on Valentine's Day is too on the nose. It's not that far away, but I'd like to think we'll still be a thing by then.

I've never gotten anyone Valentine's Day flowers before.

"Oh, and your mom came into the shop," Shay says.

I swerve slightly out of my lane. "Jesus, warn a guy before a jump scare like that."

"What? She was...nice," he says.

My palms are instantly sweaty on the steering wheel. "What did she want? I mean, how did it go?"

"Relax, we barely talked. She just poked around, told me the centerpiece number for the wedding."

I relax minutely, and then Shay adds, "I told her I knew you."

"Oh." I try to sound like I'm not panicking.

"I didn't tell her we were dating or anything."

Just like that, my heart's beating faster for a different reason. "We're dating?" I ask hesitantly.

"Yeah. Aren't we?"

"Yes, we are definitely, definitely dating," I say, because I'm not going to screw this night up like the last one. I want to date Shay. But there's a part of me that knows I'm setting myself up for trouble. I haven't told him that I haven't let my family know about him, or that the reason for that is because I'm not out to them.

I should probably come clean, but then we're at the restaurant and I let myself off the hook, at least until we've got food in our bellies.

"What's this place? I've never been here before."

"I did some research and according to the good people of the internet they supposedly have authentic tamales. They even have vegetarian ones. I thought we could give them a try."

He brightens. "Wow. That's so thoughtful—thanks, Connor."

"They might suck," I caution him. "If so, we can console ourselves with margaritas."

"I like a man with a back-up plan."

THE TAMALES DON'T SUCK.

The margaritas don't either. We stop ourselves after one each, since I have to drive, and Shay has to work tomorrow. We talk about everything and nothing as we eat in the cozy dining room. It's not fancy, but the food is fresh and delicious. It's the best date I've been on in... maybe ever. It feels like I'm out to dinner with a friend, a gorgeous friend I'm going to hopefully have really hot sex with later.

But there's more, a sort of indefinable layer to our interactions that makes me realize what I've been missing in my other friends-with-benefits situations. I wasn't really that close to those people. I didn't actually care that much what they thought of me, and I wouldn't have asked them for advice or help. But I know I could ask Shay for help and he'd do whatever he could. And I'd do the same for him.

And more, I need Shay to want me as much as I want him.

"Dessert?" I ask.

Shay laughs. "Well, I'm really full, but I will confess I picked up some pecan bars earlier. They're at my place, if you want a nightcap there."

"That's the best news I've heard all day." I'm pretty sure pecan bars mean sex. Maybe even pecan bars *and* sex. The best of all possible worlds, truly.

I pick up the check, because this is my party, and Shay's gracious about letting me.

On the drive back to his place, he asks me about the vet business. "When did your mom open her practice?"

"Oh, I was five or six? So over twenty years ago. She'd been working in another veterinary office but then the local vet in Rosedale retired and she decided to open her own practice."

"What does your dad do?"

"He's an accountant. He works from home, does the

taxes for half the businesses in Rosedale, including the books for the vet's office. His schedule was more flexible growing up, so he was the one in charge of us after school, and he made sure dinner was on the table."

"Good cook?"

"Yeah, actually. Wish his skills had rubbed off on me."

"You can still learn, if you want."

"Maybe. Do you like to cook?"

"Yes, but my apartment kitchen is so tiny I feel like a giant trying to make food in one of those plastic playhouse kitchens. I don't cook as much as I'd like to. Someday I'd love to have a house with a vegetable garden and some fruit trees, and a greenhouse of my own."

"That fits," I say, imagining Shay harvesting his own tomatoes and cucumbers, apples and pears. It's a mouthwatering image, in more ways than one.

"And the vet's office has been in this space the whole time?"

"Yes. It's a great location."

"I know. What used to be in the empty space next to me? Do you remember?"

I think back. "Maybe a shoe store? Yeah. I remember my mom making me buy penny loafers there for the holidays. I hated them with a passion."

Shay chuckles. "Not your style?"

"I lived in sneakers."

"Sporty, huh?"

"I did baseball, basketball, and soccer in school. Not particularly good at any of them, but there was always the expectation that I'd do a sport. I wouldn't say I'm a natural. I work out, though—treadmill, spinning, a little lifting when I can."

"I am, sadly, not sporty," Shay says. "I like hiking, though. There are some beautiful hikes not far from Rosedale. It's a little cold now, but in the spring, we should go."

Spring seems awfully far away, but I like the idea of getting Shay out into nature. He'd belong there, among the trees. I could kiss him in the dappled light.

"Sounds fun." I can't remember the last time I went on an actual hike, but that doesn't mean I wouldn't like it.

"So, a shoe store. Why'd it close, I wonder?"

"Probably online shopping," I suggest. "Why?"

"Oh, just thinking about our block. I'm trying to— never mind."

"What?"

There's a silence, and then Shay says, "Rodney's selling the property."

I turn onto Linden Street and go around to park in the back of our building, next to Shay's delivery van. "Oh?"

"And I'm trying to figure out a way to buy it."

NINETEEN
SHAY

I WAIT until we're inside my apartment and have shed our coats and boots before I let Connor in on my plan, or lack thereof. "I've been working the numbers all week to see if I can swing it. I almost have all the paperwork filled out to apply for a bank loan. It would be so cool to own the flower shop outright and I'm getting excited about the idea of owning the building, too. But it's a reach for me—I'm not going to lie."

"That would mean you'd be my mom's landlord," he says.

The thought had occurred to me. "Yeah, is that weird?"

"Not weird. It's just—you're really serious about Rosedale, aren't you?"

I look him in the eyes. "I really am. I know that if this doesn't work out, I'll have to pivot, find something else to do, maybe somewhere else to build a business. But I'd want to do it here."

"Wow. Okay." Connor rubs his mouth. "Well, then I hope it works out for you. Even if it means you'll be my mom's landlord." He gives me a hesitant smile.

"I was wondering—" I shouldn't ask, because I probably don't want to know the answer.

But Connor looks at me, eyes wide and expression open. "What?"

"Your mom—you haven't mentioned me to her, right?"

He immediately glances away. "No, I haven't. We don't talk about much, actually."

"Why is that? I can't get my mom to stop talking to me," I joke weakly.

"My mom—she's kind of the stereotypical flinty New Englander."

"She was a little frosty."

"That's just her way. It's nothing personal," Connor says. "But there is something I've been meaning to mention to you."

"Okay." I wait, but Connor doesn't say anything. He fiddles with a button on his shirtsleeve, and I suddenly get nervous. What is he going to say? Am I getting dumped only hours after we decided we're officially dating?

He stands up abruptly. "What about those pecan bars?'

"Oh, yeah." I get up, too, and locate the box from the Cookie Counter, opening it to reveal two glossy pecan bars that give off an intoxicating aroma of brown sugar and nuts.

"Thanks," he says, taking one but not eating it.

"Tea?"

"Please. The chamomile I got from the store doesn't taste as good as your homemade stuff."

I fill the kettle and am getting reusable tea bags out of my tea caddy when he says, "So the thing is, I'm not out to my family."

I drop the wooden box on the table with a loud clack. "Sorry. I—uh. How is that possible?" I try to make my voice as neutral as I can.

He sets the pecan bar back in the box untasted. I measure out my chamomile blend into two tea bags. Focusing on the tea preparation grounds me while I wait for him to explain.

"Would you believe it just never came up?"

"Not really," I answer honestly.

"I'm only sort of kidding," he says. "My family isn't the kind that talks about deep things or their feelings or anything like that. My mom was raised by stoic New Englanders to be a stoic New Englander. She saves her compassion for the animals at her practice." He sounds only a fraction as bitter as I would if my mom bestowed all her love elsewhere. "And I'm the emotional black sheep in my family, in that I have emotions. Even my sister's kind of an ice princess. We're just different. I learned not to bother expressing my feelings, because I'd be met with blank stares."

"Okay. Not talking about emotions is one issue, but this is who you are."

"It honestly never came up in any direct way. I

always told myself if they asked me, 'Connor, are you gay?' I'd be able to say yes. But they never did. And I guess part of me never wanted them to see me differently. I was always the kid who did everything that was expected. Good grades, sports, friends with the 'right' kids at school." He sighs unhappily and my heart goes out to him, even though I'm still confused.

"Becoming a vet?" I ask. "Is that just part of you conforming to their expectations?"

"Not exactly. I always loved visiting my mom at her office. I loved watching her work. I got to see a side of her I never saw at home. And I love being a vet now."

The bitchy comment rolls off my tongue before I can stop it. "Well, then, your *entire* life isn't a lie." His face scrunches up and I know I've hurt him. "Shit, never mind. I don't know why I said that."

"I never lied, exactly, or I try not to," he says. "It's not like I'm making up some fake girlfriend to trot out to them. I just don't talk about that side of my life, and they don't ask. When I say it never came up—I never had any kind of connection to my queer life here in Rosedale. No queer friends, certainly no prospects. It was easier than you think to keep all of that sealed off whenever I came home."

I raise my eyebrows and pour hot water over the tea bags, then hand him his mug of fragrant chamomile while I let mine steep on the countertop. I'm not sure I believe he can be twenty-eight and his family has no idea whatsoever. But then again, I've only met his mom for a minute and had one consult about flowers with his sister and her soon-to-be-husband a couple of months ago. I don't know them at all. And it sounds like I'm never going to get to know them.

My heart sinks as I realize what this means. For us.

"So you aren't out to your family, but now Meadow, Melissa, Jack, they all know." And there's me, I want to add, but this is about Connor.

"I know I have to tell them," he says quietly. "The longer I stay in Rosedale, it'll be untenable. You may not believe this, but I don't want to lie to them. To anybody. It probably sounds cowardly to you, but I'm living with them right now, I'm working for my mom. It's not like I don't have anything to lose if they don't take it well."

"Hey, first of all, I don't think you're cowardly, Connor. And I would never ask you to come out before you're totally ready. But I have to be honest—I don't know if I..." I think about Ben briefly before stuffing him back into his corner of my mind. "I really like you," I continue, "but I think you know keeping this side of my life separate from any other part of my life is impossible for me. I can't really do that, and I don't want to. So it's just going to be hard for me to keep—" I swallow hard because the idea of us breaking things off here, when they were starting to get so good, makes me unbearably sad. "To keep things on the down-low. You're awesome. If we keep dating, I'm going to want to brag about it to everyone."

He smiles faintly. "I really like you, too. And I know I'm being the baby here. I guess—give me some time?"

"I can do that," I say carefully, even though inside I'm

screaming to ask how much time he's going to need, exactly. A week? A month? Six months?

Even if we weren't together in six months, I'd still want him to feel as if he could be his whole self. I'd still want his stupid family to love him for who he is.

"Do you think they'd really give you a hard time about it?" I ask. I have some friends with horror stories, but I have more whose families were great, and it didn't turn out to be the big deal they thought it was going to be. "I mean, maybe they already know and just haven't said anything about it."

He shakes his head. "I honestly don't know. I don't think so? To either. I guess I just haven't wanted to find out if they were going to disappoint me. What's weird about it is I always figured if I had someone important in my life, someone, um, like you, it would be easier? That if I had someone concrete to point to, 'hey, here's my boyfriend,' then the words would come. But they haven't."

I take a belated sip of my cooling tea to hide my smile.

"Not that we're boyfriends, I mean this was kind of our first date," he hastens to add, his cheeks going pink under his scruff. "Obviously we're not—"

"Pecan bars," I interrupt him to save him from himself. I push the box toward him and say, "Pecan bars were our first date, actually. Then there was game night. An impromptu date, but it ended in bed, so it counts in my book. We won't count the Art Center, but that makes this our third date. And on the third date, you're allowed to decide if you're boyfriends or not."

"Oh, you are?" His shy smile hits me in the solar plexus.

"Yes, according to the handbook of relationship rules I just made up."

He comes around to my side of the table, puts his arm around my waist. "You're not pissed about this?"

"I'm not pissed about it. But I'm going to be honest and say I think you'd probably feel better if you told them, if only to not have to be thinking about it all the time."

"You are the kind of person who says what they think, aren't you," he says, and it sounds more admiring than annoyed, which is good.

"I can't help it, actually."

"Good." He kisses me then, as if rewarding me for my candor. "I'm going to try to channel that more."

I kiss him back lightly. "Yeah? What are you thinking right now?"

"I'm thinking I want to take your hair out of this." He touches the elastic holding my hair in a ponytail. "I love your hair."

I reach up and pull the elastic free, shaking my hair to cover my neck. "That's a coincidence because I love your hair, too." I put my hands into the thick thatch and tug lightly, bringing him in for another kiss, deeper this time.

He groans and rubs his growing erection against the front of my crotch. My cock stirs in response. "It's my best feature."

"Mmmm. It's great hair. But it's only one of the front runners for your best feature," I argue. "There are your eyes," I press light kisses to each of his eyelids, "and your mouth." I kiss him there, snake my hands under his shirt, and scratch my nails over his nipples. He yelps, and I smile. "So many best features."

"Thanks," he replies breathlessly. "You wanna do a complete inventory?"

"Definitely." And we leave the pecan bars and tea behind to go to bed.

TWENTY

CONNOR

GETTING into bed with Shay this time is looser than the first night. We know each other better, and the comfort level means I don't have to rely on the tried-and-true moves I use when I'm hooking up with a guy for the first time and the main objective is to simply get each other off.

Now I can do things I know Shay likes because I'm learning his body. We're still getting to know each other, but we've passed from the initial stranger stage to a place where we can be more ourselves because we've built up some trust.

I told him I wasn't out, and he didn't freak. He didn't lie and say everything was peachy, either. I know he wants me to tell my family. But that's a problem for another day.

Tonight, I'm going to enjoy my good fortune of having someone gorgeous, smart, funny and supportive in my bed. Well, his bed.

Maybe one day I'll have it together enough to invite him into mine.

We take off our clothes, then dive under the covers, the room's slanted ceiling holding us close as we touch and kiss and explore. Shay changed his barbells out for hoops sometime since I last saw his naked chest. I make it my mission to see how much he can take when I'm worrying the hoops between my teeth, tugging and licking up every spark of pleasure. He arches up, a sighing, groaning mess by the time I leave his pleasingly pink nipples to latch my mouth around the head of his cock.

I can't stop running my hands over his smooth skin, his torso a mile long and his endless legs wrapping around me as I take him down as far as I can.

"Connor, god." He sounds wrecked. I glance up his long body and our eyes meet. His gaze looks green to me now as he smiles down at me. "Fuck, you look hot." I literally swallow down a thank you, my tongue and throat working around his hard cock, and he shouts, "Fuck! So good." I let him buck into my mouth a few times, the smooth slide and the ache in my jaw turning me on. I pump my own length a few times.

"You touching yourself?" Shay asks. There's not much room between the mattress and Shay holding me close to him, but enough to get a rhythm going. I nod. "Fuck, that's hot." He makes a frustrated noise and curls up so he can tug lightly at my hair. "Hey, come up here."

I let his cock go with a wet pop and run my tongue over my lips, which feel pleasantly bee-stung.

"Yeah, come here, sexy," he says, and I oblige, shuffling

up the bed. He kisses me and wraps his long-fingered hand around my shaft at the same time. My chest rumbles on a long moan. It feels amazing to shower attention on him, but when that attention gets redirected my way, it's total sensory overload. He bombards me with pleasure, kissing me so fiercely I can feel it in my balls, which are tight and full and ready to spill over his expert hand, which he's using to draw the orgasm out of me with slow, sure strokes.

"So sexy," he murmurs between kisses, "with your mouth full of my cock."

"Tastes good," I confide, settling back into his pillows, so I'm half sitting up. I pull at his hips to get him to climb on top of me. "You like getting sucked?"

He laughs breathlessly. "Who doesn't?"

"Let me suck it again." I remember how hot it was last week when he told me to come on his nipples. "Finish in my mouth."

He swears enthusiastically, rising up on his knees so his cock bobs right in front of my face. I look up at him through my lashes and he swears again, grabbing his cock at the base and feeding it to me slowly. I'm not blowing smoke—his cock tastes good, fresh and clean, and it fills me up just right. I get it about halfway in, then use my hand to jack the base while he stutters forward and back with small movements of his hips. His hair's hanging messy in his face as he looks down at me, his lips parted.

I'm hard enough that any touch feels like it's going to finish me off, so I wait as long as I can before I get my other hand around myself, reaching through Shay's legs to stroke myself off.

"Touching yourself again? Fuck, Connor, yes, I'm

going to finish in your gorgeous mouth, sexy." He's good as his word, grunting as his jizz floods my mouth, sharp and tangy on my tongue. His come doesn't taste as velvety sweet as his cock, but it's not bad, and I swallow because I don't have the wherewithal to do anything else. My own orgasm is frustratingly elusive, focused as I am on wringing the last drops out of Shay, but then he pulls himself free of my mouth, swings his leg over, and helps me out. The sensation of his big elegant hand over my sturdy smaller one, both of us jacking me from root to tip, sends me over the edge and I tense up so hard my teeth grind together as my climax finally erupts.

"So sexy," Shay croons as I'm coming down from the high, hand and stomach a sopping mess. He leans down and kisses me, pulling away with a wrinkled nose. "You swallowed."

"Told you, you taste good." I have what feels like a Cheshire Cat grin on my face as I take the wad of tissues Shay hands me and clean myself up as best I can.

Shay pulls on his boxer briefs. "You want to take a shower?"

A yawn is my answer as exhaustion from the night and the entire long week catches up with me. "Later."

He smiles. "Okay, I'll be right back."

I'm only most of the way asleep when he comes back to bed, shutting the light off on his way. We snuggle into the cocoon of blankets. The bed hasn't gotten any bigger since the last time we shared it, but it feels easier to slide into a comfortable position, me as little spoon this time. "Is it okay if I stay over?" I whisper into the dark.

"Of course." There's a pause in which I contemplate

actually falling asleep, but then he says, "Your parents won't worry?"

Guilt churns in my gut. "I, uh, told my dad I might stay out."

"Oh." Shay manages to sound confused in that single syllable, and I don't blame him.

This can't go on, obviously. I want to promise him that I'll fix this, that I'll correct ten plus years of omission and just tell them already, but he speaks first.

"I'm glad you're here, Connor." He presses his forehead into my upper back. "I want to tell you something, though."

My tiredness falls away as the adrenaline spike at his words has me instantly alert. "What's that?"

"I thought you should know, in case I seemed weird about the whole not being out thing. My ex, uh, Ben. That was his name." He's talking into my back, and I stay stock still to ensure I don't miss a word. "He, well, it wasn't that he wasn't out. But he had a lot of secrets. He kept a lot back from me. Kept me out of a lot of his life. He'd invite me in, then push me away, and, well, it kind of gave me some trust issues. So I'm glad you told me, even if you don't—um, I know it's not easy. I'm not explaining myself very well. I just want you to know that I might seem like I have it all together—hah—but I've got some issues, too. So. Yeah. That's it."

Shay does seem like he has it all together, at least outside of work, but his speech is a good reminder that we're all continually figuring ourselves out.

"Thanks for sharing that with me," I say. "He

shouldn't have treated you like that." I hate the thought of anyone's trust being abused, but especially Shay's.

His forehead leaves my back, and he rolls over—away from me. I turn and make out the line of him in the dark. I touch his shoulder through the thin tee he wore to bed. "Hey, are you okay?"

"Yeah."

He doesn't sound particularly okay.

I sit all the way up. "Shay." I'm out of my depth, not used to late night heart-to-hearts or dealing with the issues of a partner because I've never really had one before.

Thankfully, Shay throws me a lifeline. He's good at that. "I haven't talked about Ben in a long time. I sort of put him in this box and I put the box away and I try never to think about him."

He turns over again and I see his face in the light filtering in from the streetlamp through the window under the eve.

Something occurs to me, and I bring it up before I can think it through. "Do you still have feelings for him?"

In addition to hating someone who hurt Shay, I can now add jealous of the jerk to my list of character flaws.

But Shay's response comes gratifyingly quickly. "No —no. He'd break up with me when I tried to get closer, then come sweeping back in weeks later and pretend nothing had happened. I went along with it because I thought I loved him. But he never actually let me close enough to see the real him. I never even met his parents in the three years we were off-and-on."

"Three years?" That sounds like a long time. But I listen to what he's really saying. This Ben character didn't let Shay fully into his life, jerked him around to suit his own needs. I'm just as bad as him, even if my motives are different.

"He was very charming," Shay says. "We had a lot of chemistry. It made it easy to ignore the things about him that weren't so great. When I finally ended things, he was —ugly. That's when I decided to leave Scottsdale, and I found this place."

"You were running away."

"Kind of. But I'd like to think I was giving myself an opportunity to heal, to find out who I was without him hanging over my head. My family, too. They're really great, for the most part, but they're overbearing. I needed to discover who I was on my own. And I have. And now I've found you and I guess...I'm scared everything's going to go away. The flower shop. You. My life in Rosedale. It all seems so precarious, but I want it so much."

I want to reassure him, but I don't know how. "It's a good thing that you're scared to lose these things," I say. "It means you have the right things in your life. The important things."

"Yeah. But it's scary."

Scary. No shit. I'm terrified that he's counting me among the parts of his life he doesn't want to lose when I'm both getting more attached to him by the second and yet have no idea what my own future holds. But I'm here right now. And I can stay, for the night, anyway. "Hey, you built this great life here from scratch. Even if things do change, you can do it again if you have to."

He hums as if he finds my paltry words encouraging.

"Thanks for listening. It's nice to have someone who cares. I've been doing it on my own for a while. And before that, Ben was never really there for me the way I wanted him to be. So thanks, Connor."

My chest swells with pride at giving Shay something he hasn't been able to get from anyone else.

"I'm happy to listen. It might be the only thing I can do, but I'll do it gladly."

Impulsively, I lean forward and kiss him. He tastes like toothpaste, and I realize I was so blissed out from the sex that I didn't even use the toothbrush I brought like a good little scout.

"I forgot to brush my teeth. I'll go—"

"No, wait," Shay says, and he deepens the kiss, apparently not minding my breath.

We kiss for a long time in the dark, then we fall asleep with our arms around each other under the warmth of his quilt.

I end up not using the toothbrush until the morning.

THE WEEKEND after our tamale date is about as perfect a weekend as I've had since coming to Rosedale. It's an off week for game night, so after a busy Saturday at the shop, Connor comes over with takeout. We talk and eat on my couch, then don't even bother with the pretense of a movie or anything and go to bed, where we trade blow jobs and kisses until the early morning.

Sunday is the only day of the week that we both have off, but Connor is on-call, so we can't go anywhere particularly far away. We opt to stay in bed late, talking and laughing, until the need for caffeine and food rousts us and I make French toast. I laugh when Connor's eyes roll back in his head in appreciation.

"It's so simple to make," I tell him. "I'll show you next time."

I'm on a sugar high from the maple syrup, but his wide excited smile makes my pulse race even faster. "I'd like that."

The weather is cold and dry. We bundle up and go

for a walk on the local trail that starts in the old cemetery on the edge of downtown, then hit up Hot Brew for drinks to warm us up from the inside. We browse the secondhand store—I find a vintage metal trough that's perfect for a display in the shop, and Connor buys a small porcelain figurine of a white dog he says reminds him of his family's dog Snowy and will make a good wedding gift for his sister.

The problem of the flower shop and the loan is in the back of my mind all the time, but I don't want to ruin what's a perfect day off with my work worries. We don't talk about the heavy stuff we brought up Friday, either, but I can tell that sharing those things with each other has brought us closer.

We hit up more friends at their workplaces. Melissa chats with us for a while at the bookshop, then we go to the Cookie Counter. Beck's not working today, but we still get cookies for later from his employee. Finally, we duck into McGinty's, the Irish pub, for a late lunch-slash-early dinner.

Connor hasn't explicitly said we shouldn't advertise that we're not just two bros out for a day in Rosedale, but I'm acutely aware that he wouldn't want to be outed to his parents by someone telling them they saw him holding hands with a boy, so I keep my twitching fingers to myself. This is such a small town, though, that I privately think he's delusional if he believes he can keep up a relationship with me and hide it from his parents for much longer.

Then it's back to bed, where we kiss and give each other hand jobs. I'm ready to turn in and tuck Connor against me, but then he informs me he can't stay over for a third night in a row. He has to work in the morning, after all. I have to let go of the vision of waking up with him, kissing him good morning, and making him tea before sending him off to work. But just because the shop is closed on Mondays doesn't mean I don't have work to do, either. I'm ready to submit the last of my paperwork to the bank before I start crossing all my fingers and maybe even some toes.

WITH VALENTINE'S DAY APPROACHING, the shop is busy, so Connor and I don't see each other much during the week. He manages to stop by one day on his lunch break, looking cute as hell in his scrubs. Lucky for us, the shop is empty just then, so I pull him out of sight behind the refrigerator case and we make out for a couple of minutes, laughing like we're getting away with something. I send him back to work with flushed cheeks and a semi, which he tucks into his waistband.

Friday's the first night we can commit to a proper date. I told him it was my turn to plan it, and that he should come over after closing. I'm distracted all day, thinking about having him to myself all night. I've missed him in my bed, snuggling under the covers with me. I don't know what he told his family to explain needing to crash elsewhere for two consecutive nights, and I didn't ask. I'm happy to keep living in this perfect bubble for a while longer. I know it won't last, but I don't want to end it prematurely.

I don't want this thing with Connor to end, period.

He's the whole package, offering the kind of grown-up relationship I'm actually ready for at almost thirty. The type of man I could easily see being my partner for the rest of my life. He's smart, romantic, capable, and yes, in his own words, good in bed.

I can tell by the smile I can't seem to ever fully wipe off my face that I'm falling for him.

Is it perfect? Not by a long shot. What future can we have if he's still got one foot back in Chicago and he's working for his mother who doesn't even know I exist, outside of being the person who's furnishing flowers for her daughter's wedding?

I'm getting pretty good at not dwelling on things I don't want to think about when a coatless man with a wild-eyed expression comes into the flower shop after lunch on Friday, pinging my danger antennae.

"Can I help you?" I ask, moving out from behind the counter and wiping my hands, wet from finalizing a funeral arrangement, on my apron.

"Um. I'm not actually in the market for flowers. I was just looking for a temporary escape."

"Oh, well, this is a good place for that," I say, trying to keep it light. He seems harmless so far, but you never know. "Mind if I ask what you're escaping from? Do I need to call the cops or something?"

He laughs at that and relaxes a bit. He's wearing a sweater and thermal hiking pants. The sweater molds to his chest, and there's something vaguely familiar about his boy-next-door face. "No, nothing like that. I was touring the space next door, and I got a little panicky."

"Oh?" Touring the space next door—that means he's thinking of renting it. "What's your business?"

"I'm thinking of opening up a bike shop. Bike sales, repairs, that kind of thing."

I mull it over, picturing having a bike shop as my direct neighbor, and what it means if all the spots in this building are occupied. It makes buying it more feasible than before, since I could count on rent from three units. I give my approval, and he talks about how he's nervous about opening a business, which I get. Then I finally put two and two together. He's the guy who organized a charity bike event last fall that I donated to, and he's friends with Jack and Pete.

"Yep," he confirms. "Charlie Linden."

"I'm Shay Brierley. And this is Linden Street. It's a sign." I smile at him, wanting to make a good impression if we're going to be neighbors. And if I might possibly become his landlord.

We chat for another minute until a man walks in holding a jacket and looking worried. It turns out this is Charlie's boyfriend, Drew. I get them to buy a plant and try not to intrude on their private moment when they seem to be coming to terms with the major step of Charlie taking the plunge on this bike shop business. Their banter and the easy way they are with each other, not afraid to touch in public—I love to see it, and I'm pleased they feel the flower shop is a safe space for that.

After they leave, I call Daryl at the bank. He confirms that he got all my paperwork but says it'll take a few more business days to get any answers for me. I drum my fingers on the counter but try not to transfer my anxiety through the phone. There's nothing for me to do but be patient, but it's hard when I know for certain now this is what I want.

And Connor is, too.

I shoot him a quick text.

> Thinking about you. Looking forward to tonight.

I went out last night after work to get the ingredients for our dinner, so all I have to do once I flip the open sign to closed on the shop's door is head upstairs and spruce myself up. I did laundry this week, so I make sure the bed is neat and tidy, that the lube and condoms are in reach. I have some ideas about how the evening will end, and we'll be needing those if Connor agrees.

I take out the wine I bought from Ariana at Wine and Roses earlier in the week, pulling out the tumblers I use for wine glasses and setting them on the table. Maybe I should actually break down and buy real wine glasses now that I have a regular wine-drinking guest.

My apartment feels even smaller since Connor started hanging out here. It was never all that big to begin with, but it was adequate. If I buy the building, maybe I could save up enough over the next few years to buy a real house. Rosedale isn't as pricey as some of the surrounding towns, but it's not exactly cheap. But the dream of having a real home, a bigger kitchen, a garden of my own—it's powerful. And now Connor's in the picture, too. I know he'd love to have a pet. Maybe we could get a rescue dog.

No, I scold myself. Bad Shay. It's only been a few

weeks. Sheesh. I've tried not getting ahead of myself, but clearly my imagination is running away with me.

Connor may be everything I want, but we still need to take it one day, one date at a time.

Speaking of dates, I check my watch. Where is my date? He's late, and there are no messages on my phone. I push aside the tendril of unease and go to chop vegetables for the stir-fry.

TWENTY-TWO
CONNOR

FRIDAY AFTERNOON we have a couple of
cancelations, so Violet and I finish up on the early side.
I'm stoked, because that means I can run back to the
house and shower before meeting Shay. He'd made the
plans for tonight, wouldn't tell me what they are, just
instructed me to meet him at his place after work.

"You look happy," Violet comments as I rush through
the closing routine. "And your mom says you've been out
a lot of nights."

"So?"

"So, what's her name?"

Fuck. "There's no her," I say lightly, not wanting to
get into a whole thing. "I'm allowed to be happy,
aren't I?"

"Of course. It's been great to see so much of you this
winter, Connor. Just—"

"You think it's been going well?" I ask, quickly
changing the subject to work.

"Definitely. A few hiccups, but the patients have given lots of positive feedback. You've been doing a wonderful job. Your mom thinks so, too."

"That's good to hear." It would be nice to hear it from her, but I'll take it second hand if that's all I'm going to get.

"You should really consider staying on after her arm heals up. The two of you could make a good team."

"Is this your idea or hers?" I know Mom brought it up in an oblique way the other day, but she hasn't mentioned it since then.

"It's common sense. She's got a lot of good working years left, but having a second full-time vet on staff would make life easier for everyone. I'm sure we could afford it because we'd be able to take on new patients."

"Well, I'll think about it," I say. "If she offers it to me."

"Connor Nieves, sometimes you have to ask for what you want, not wait for someone to give it to you."

She leaves before I can respond to that. I'm just happy to have gotten her off the subject of girls. I try not to feel like a failure for not taking the opportunity to tell her the reason for the perpetual smile on my face is Shay.

When I make it home, it's already dark. My dad's car is gone, but my sister's SUV is sitting in the driveway. I clunk through the front door, ready to make a beeline for the shower, but I detour to the kitchen when my sister calls out a greeting.

Courtney's at the kitchen island, head bent over a hand-drawn picture of the reception tables, and glances up when I come in. Snowy's on his dog bed. He lifts his head and thumps his tail a few times when he sees me. I crouch down and give him a vigorous pat and a kiss on the nose. He sniffs me vigorously, too, no doubt smelling ten different animals on me.

"Glad you're here," Courtney says. "Do you think it's a bad idea to sit Dad's sister with Mom's Uncle Jasper? I don't want them arguing over politics."

"Uh. Probably."

"Dammit." She crosses something out, writes something down. "Mom and Violet did their best with this, but I can't stop tinkering with it. What's up with you?"

"Just came home to shower and change."

Courtney looks surprised. "Oh, you have plans? I thought maybe we could grab dinner. Mike's at a conference and Mom and Dad are having dinner with some friends."

"I do have plans." I feel bad; I've barely seen my sister since I got to town. Tomorrow night is game night, this time to be held at Melissa and Meadow's place. Courtney would probably have fun there, but that would involve doing the thing I've been meaning to do and haven't found the courage to actually do.

"Oh. Okay." She looks down at the seating chart. "God, I'll be so happy when this wedding is over. It's been like a second job."

"Only a few more days now," I say to encourage her.

"Two weeks from today."

So soon. I think about how good Shay would look dressed up for a wedding. I bet he'd look amazing in a suit, his long hair pulled back, his slim waist in trim pants. It would be so hot knowing he's got those damn tantalizing piercings underneath his clothes.

Would it be so unthinkable to bring him to the wedding?

I've barely allowed myself to entertain the idea when I catch Courtney's expression. Her forehead is all wrinkled, and she says, "You look...happy."

"Thanks?" I make it a question, since she didn't exactly make being happy seem like a good thing.

"I just haven't seen you like this in a long time. When you came home these last few years, you always seemed stressed."

I'm surprised she noticed. "Well, I was in a stressful program," I say. "Working is actually easier than being in school."

"How is work, by the way?"

"It's...good. Mom hasn't been micromanaging, which I appreciate. The workload is on the heavy side, but I like to keep busy. I don't know how she does it all herself, honestly."

"Have you thought about, I don't know, staying on?"

"Staying on at Mom's?"

"Yeah." Courtney smiles. "It would be nice to have you here all the time. And Mom could use the help. And you'd have a full-time job."

"I've thought about it. Violet mentioned the idea, too." It used to be my dream to work with Mom in her practice. And staying in Rosedale would mean being able to be with Shay. I'd be a grown up with a real job and a real relationship. No more hiding behind school and inconsequential hookups.

But staying in Rosedale would mean reconciling the person I've become with the person my family thinks I am.

My heart sinks. I'm only torturing myself by imagining Shay dressed up for the wedding. I'm not taking him as my date if I can't even tell my sister that the person I have plans with tonight is him.

"Well, Mom would love it," Courtney says, and it takes me a second to remember what we were talking about.

"Maybe."

"So, you have the bachelor party on your calendar, right? It's next Sunday."

"Uh. Right."

"You have to go; you promised to make sure nothing crazy happens."

"Right, I remember." I pull out my phone to double check I really do have it in my calendar and see a text from Shay. It's much later than I thought. "Damn."

"What's wrong?" Courtney asks.

"I—I'm late for my dinner plans."

"Plans with who?"

I open my mouth, then close it. If I tell her it's Shay, there will be more questions. But if I don't tell her, I might as well not go over to Shay's at all. He deserves more than what I've been able to give him.

A wave of dizziness crashes over me and I sink to the ground, resting against the cold stainless-steel facade of the dishwasher. For a very real moment, I consider not telling her, just continuing to be only part of myself when I'm home, not being my real self with my family, the people I love most in the world. The idea of being that big of a coward, that willing to trade a bit of privacy in exchange for my authenticity, makes me even more nauseous than imagining the fallout from just saying his name.

If my sister had walked away, or stayed where she was, I might have let myself get away with it. But she sinks down to kneel next to me, not touching, but close enough I see the facets of her diamond ring.

"Shay Brierley." His name tastes good on my tongue and returns some of my strength. "The florist?"

"I know Shay," she says evenly. She doesn't sound surprised, or judgmental, or curious. She just waits.

"We have dinner plans." It's easier to reveal small chunks of information. "We're dating."

She doesn't react, except to say, "Oh."

I take a breath. She'd let me get away with only saying that. But I have to say the rest. "I'm gay."

I've said it out loud to other people before, to friends and lovers. I've known it since I was sixteen. But I've never said it to someone whose rejection would really hurt.

My sister smiles, like this is good news. "Thanks for telling me." Then she gets up on her knees and puts her arms around me.

I hug her back, hard, because I'd built this up in my head so much that her reaction is anticlimactic. But in a good way. "Thanks," I whisper. I want to cry. I probably should cry. But we're still Nieveses. Courtney can probably handle my being gay more easily than me crying on her shoulder.

She squeezes me one more time for good measure before letting go. Snowy pads over from his bed to see what we're doing on the floor, noses us curiously until I start scratching behind his ears. His soft fur makes me feel grounded—a pet's unconditional love is always a welcome balm to whatever hurts.

Telling Courtney didn't hurt, though. It just reminded me how much I love my sister.

"You haven't told Mom and Dad," she says calmly.

"I need to tell them, obviously," I say. "I always planned to tell them when there was a reason to. Like when I met someone. But then I never met anyone, and that plan never panned out." I sigh.

"Well, life doesn't always go according to plan," Courtney says like the teacher she is.

"Thanks," I say dryly.

"Besides, you've met someone now."

Shay's face flashes in my brain, attractive and opinionated and kind. "I have met someone. And I should tell Mom and Dad." I blow out a frustrated breath. "It's not easy to talk about personal stuff with them, is it?"

She laughs shortly. "Mom and Dad are a little repressed. Hell, count me in, too."

I wonder what feelings and secrets she's been carrying around instead of sharing them. I feel like a bad brother because I've kept her at arm's length instead of letting her know all of me.

"I'm sorry."

"For what?" She sounds honestly baffled, which makes me feel worse.

"I haven't been there. I haven't been *here*. Because it was easier for me to stay away."

"Hey, I don't blame you for anything. Bottom line, you have to do what you feel is best for you."

"Thanks."

"But if you stayed away from Rosedale, from me, because you didn't feel like you could be yourself at home, well. I miss you." She says it matter-of-factly, but I can sense the hurt behind her words. "Maybe you could just not live with Mom and Dad, for starters?"

I laugh. "Yeah. Okay. That's a good place to begin. I've actually really enjoyed getting to know Rosedale these last few weeks. It feels different than when I was in high school. It feels—safe."

"That's important. You should feel safe at home. And Rosedale is your home. You belong here as much as anyone."

I consider her words. For the first time in a long time, I actually feel like I do belong here. I get to my feet and put a hand out to help Courtney up. I stretch to my full height—okay, it's not that high, but whatever. It feels good to be in my body, my feet on the ground, my sister seeing me, and me allowing her to see me, all of me.

"So, Shay," she says with a small smile. "He's very attractive."

"Court!" I wrinkle my nose in her direction.

"What? I like a good man bun." She grins.

I laugh. "I better go. I'm already super late."

She gives me one more hug. Are we a hugging family now? "Have a good night."

"Thanks." Impulsively, I say, "Love you."

She looks surprised for the first time tonight. "Love you, too," she says, her cheeks pink.

I'm out to her and the world hasn't changed. I'm still me. The Nieves siblings are still emotionally constipated, but we're working on it. And I'm still monumentally late for dinner with my new boyfriend.

TWENTY-THREE
SHAY

I'M THINKING about opening up the wine and getting a head start when I get Connor's text.

I'll be late. Will explain.

I breathe easier, finish prepping the dinner ingredients. He texts me again thirty minutes later, and I find him standing outside the back door when I go down to let him in.

Before I can say anything, he pulls me into his arms. Mine go around him instinctively. He melts into me until I'm hugging him more than he's hugging me. I stroke his hair, the cold outside air mixing with the warm air from inside. I'm not wearing enough layers for this, but I let him hold me—and hold him back—until he pulls away.

"Shay." He sniffs and I bring him all the way inside and shut the door.

"Are you okay? Did something happen?" Worry

floods my gut, but I can see for myself that he's safe and whole.

"Yeah, I, uh—can we go up?"

Once we're in the apartment, he says, "I told Courtney that I'm gay. And that you and I are seeing each other."

Relief mixed with trepidation bubbles up inside me. I'm so very glad he took that step, not least because of what it means for us, but he hasn't given any indication of how it went. "Tell me about it."

"She was really great." He blinks and there are tears gathering in the corners of his eyes.

"Oh, Connor." I pull him against my chest. "It's okay," I murmur as his breath hitches in starts and fits.

"It's a lot." A minute later, he's able to say more. "I thought about it so many times and it was just—it felt good, but man, was it scary."

I make a cooing sound. "I know."

He tells me the short version of their conversation, and I'm glad she offered him unconditional support. Plus one for Connor's family. He still has to cross this bridge with his parents, but it's a solid step in that direction. "That's so good. I'm so proud of you."

"Thanks." He blows his nose on a tissue from his pocket. "I don't know why I'm so emotional about this. I don't really cry about stuff."

I fondly smile at my sweet, repressed boyfriend. "You're emotional because it's a big freaking deal. God, I'm so proud of you," I say again, because it's too soon for the other thing that I want to say, which is that I love him.

I know I do, at least as a friend. But that's not what he needs to hear right now. "You're amazing."

"I don't think I deserve much credit. It's long overdue."

"Stop. You did it. That's what matters."

"Thanks." He wipes his eyes with his thumb. "You're too easy on me, you know?"

"I'm not going to lie. When you were late, I was a little worried." I spent too much time before getting his first text repeating the mantra that he's not Ben over and over in my head. "We need a better notification system."

"It's just that I wanted to fit in a shower before I came over. And Courtney was there, and I told her, and then I finally got in the shower, and that's why I'm late."

"It's okay," I say, brushing my own insecurities to the side. "That was more important. But I bet you're hungry."

"I am. What's all this?" he asks, indicating the chopped veggies and tofu on the counter.

"Our date. I thought I could teach you how to make something." It seems kind of silly now. "But we could put this stuff away and order—"

"No," he cuts me off. "It's a nice idea. Thanks, Shay."

"Wash your hands, then. Want a glass of wine?"

"The biggest one you have."

"On it." I pause to press a kiss to his mouth. "I am really proud of you, Connor." I hope he can feel the love coming through that kiss.

"Thanks, Shay."

We have fun making a tofu veggie stir-fry—the rice

being the hardest part for Connor to wrap his head around.

"How do you know if it's done if you can't open the lid?"

"You get a feel for the timing after you've made it a few times. And you can lift the lid, just not every two minutes," I say, batting his hand away from the pot.

Half an hour later, we're eating, sitting on the couch. "This is actually tasty." Connor sounds surprised. "And it wasn't that hard."

"Glad you think so. Next time you can take the lead and I'll be the sous chef. And then you'll be able to make it yourself."

"Wow, you have a lot of faith in my ability to learn."

"You went to veterinary school, didn't you? Making a stir-fry is easy in comparison."

"That's what you think."

We put the leftovers away, but before I can offer him any dessert, he's crowded me against the kitchen counter. With his hands boxing me in, he kisses me long and sweet. I forget all about dessert when he whispers, "Can we go to bed now?"

I nod and let him lead me there. I want him so badly, but as if by unspoken agreement, we take things slowly, stripping each other down to nothing. Connor's hands are warm on my skin. His stubble is long, only a few days' growth from transitioning to an actual beard, and when he kisses me, the soft-spiky sensation on my skin makes me shiver. His tongue is salty from the soy sauce we used to season our stir-fry.

I can't help feeling certain that this is the guy I'm

supposed to be with. He makes me feel so many things—hopeful, cared for, desired. He's got some issues, but so do I. We're not coming to this relationship as blank slates, but I like the combination we make together.

Once naked, we get horizontal because of the slanted ceiling, but Connor just sighs happily and wriggles into the sheets, pulling the quilt up and over us. "I love your bed."

I laugh a little. "Really? It's too small."

"Yeah, but you're in it."

How can I not melt at that, kiss him, and rub up against him like a cat?

"Would you be interested in fucking me tonight?" I whisper along his jaw. We've discussed our statuses—both negative, both recently tested—even though we haven't done penetrative stuff yet.

But every time we get in this bed, I just want more.

"I'm interested," he says, his finger sweeping almost unconsciously across my nipple ring. I shudder and my blood heats. "Or...you could fuck me."

TWENTY-FOUR
SHAY

I BLINK. I haven't topped in a long time. Ben hadn't been an enthusiastic bottom, even though I like to switch. God, what a dick. Why did I stay with him for so long? Not thinking about that now. I grip Connor's meaty thighs and wrap my legs around them.

"We could take turns," I suggest, wanting it all.

"I'm on board with that."

"Okay." I reach for the lube. "I asked first," I say, uncapping the lid.

"Fair's fair," he answers. He holds out his hand and I look at it, confused. He looks at me, equally lost. "You want me to prep you, right?"

"Right, sure. Be my guest." Ben always made me do it myself. I give Connor the lube, then a quick kiss, and arrange myself on the bed, legs spread. "It's been a really long time for me," I warn him. Almost two years. I tense, because it hurts to have things put inside you sometimes.

"Shay, relax." He puts a hand on my belly, and I automatically lose the tension in my hips. "Breathe." I obey, oxygen filling my lungs and filling me with calm at the same time.

Connor efficiently slicks up his fingers, then lifts my balls out of the way before circling my hole with the pads of two fingers, stimulating all my nerves without actually getting inside me.

"Wow," I say, the sensations lighting me up like a pinball machine.

"Feel good?"

I catch his gaze, liking the way he's focused completely on me. "Yeah."

He adds more lube, then unerringly slides a single finger inside me without a hint of pain. "Okay?"

I idly think that his experience with animals probably helps him with skittish boyfriends in bed. Lucky me. I'm ready to get down on my knees and worship his strong, capable hands. "Very okay."

After a while, he adds another finger. "You're really good at this," I say. I'm relaxed and open and in no pain whatsoever. "I don't even bother with toys because I'm too impatient. I never open myself up enough and some-times it hurts," I confess.

He clucks his tongue at me. "You have to tell me if I hurt you, okay?"

"I will." I feel the stretch with the third finger, and then he grazes my prostate and I suck in a breath.

He stops immediately. "Are you—"

"No, that was good—keep going." I feel like I'm prac-tically drooling, but I can't help it. "Want more."

"You can have more," he promises. "You can have whatever you want."

I shake and feel a touch of wetness where the tip of my cock scrapes my belly. I'm stiff and dripping like a popsicle on a hot day. "Connor, fuck. I want you."

He takes out his fingers, wipes them on a tissue, kisses me. I suck on his tongue in lieu of his cock, and he groans. "I gotta get the condom."

I know it's a good idea—it's less messy for one thing—but I wonder if down the road we could do without them. I already know after tonight I'm going to need Connor to take care of me like this a lot more. He can have me forever.

"Ready?" he asks. While I've been thinking rapturous thoughts, he's gotten himself gloved up, lubed up. "Is this a good position for you?"

"I'm so good," I respond languidly. My body is a contradiction. I'm so comfortable I couldn't move if the smoke detector went off, but my cock is so hard I feel like I'd come in three seconds if he wrapped his delicious hand around me and tugged.

He chuckles lightly. "Well, you look good. You look like a debauched angel, Shay."

"Ruin your angel," I urge, spreading my legs farther so he can get in there. "Please."

The first blunt pressure is a shock, but he's done such a good job of getting me slick and stretched for him that there's not even a twinge when he slides in. There's only the feeling of fullness, of my body opening up for him, taking him in, wanting to keep him there.

I lock my legs around his, holding him close. With our height difference, I have to curl over to steal a kiss, but it doesn't matter. Everything feels good. He's always turned me on, never had any trouble making me come, but right now, pumping into me, Connor really seems in his element.

"You good, angel?"

I groan at the endearment, a mingling of pleasure and embarrassment. "Yeah," I grit out. "Harder."

"You gonna come, angel? Because I want that pretty cock in me next."

I let out an unintelligible noise, keeping my hands off myself with an iron will. "TBD," I bite out. "But harder." I want to feel him lose himself in me. I want to feel that he's as overwhelmed by me as I am by him.

He speeds up, his hips snapping as he thrusts into me, strong and sure. It smells amazing, our scents earthy and fresh. The sound of skin smacking against skin is utterly arousing. A flush rises on his chest under the sparse line of dark hair dusting his pecs. His mouth is parted, his eyes set in concentration.

"Come on, sexy," I order him. "Give me everything."

He throws his head back as he jerks us forward so hard my head hits the wall. I scramble to get a pillow between me and a concussion, and he groans. "Coming, fuck, coming."

I can't exactly feel him filling the condom, but I can feel it when his movements slow and I have a chance to really experience the stretch in my ass. He's not huge, but plenty thick. He drops his chin to his chest, breathing hard. I squirm. I'm still so hard it almost hurts, but it's satisfyingly distracting to see Connor navigate his post-orgasm haze.

"Damn, Shay." He raises his head to look at me, a dopey smile on his face.

I grin back at him. "My turn?"

"Yeah, yeah," he says, carefully pulling out, his hand on the base of the condom. He takes care of it, wipes himself down.

I eagerly trade places with him, my earlier torpor gone in the face of a raging hard-on that needs release. He's loose and pliant, making it easy for me to open him up with plenty of lube and my fingers, which are thinner than his, but longer. I love the sounds he makes—moans and grunts and "more."

"I'm ready," he says, though it doesn't feel like I've quite done enough prep.

"You sure?" I look doubtfully down at him, but he doesn't seem hesitant in the least, and his cock is halfway hard, as if he might be on his way to rebounding. He urges me closer.

"Definitely, angel."

God, that nickname. My heart wars between insisting it's too much and wanting to demand he never stop calling me that.

I get another condom out, twitching my nose at the plasticky smell, one I associate with sex but have never really enjoyed.

"Okay?" I ask, triple checking.

"If you don't get your cock up my ass in the next—"

I don't wait for him to finish, but breach him while he's distracted, and god it's been so long since I've topped, I forgot what it feels like to be clutched by a tight, hot channel. It feels fucking good.

"Oh god." Connor bites his lip. "That's right, angel." Sweat breaks out on his hairline as I inch all the way inside. "Go for it," he almost grunts.

"I don't want to hurt you," I say. "You look—"

"It's intense," he says, his grip vice-tight on my arms. "But it's wonderful. Don't stop. Please."

I look down to where we're joined, and it's crazy hot because it's us. Then I notice he's harder than before, so I figure I must be doing something right. "Okay."

I pull out and slide back in and then it's just natural rhythm taking over, the sensation of claiming Connor's body sending a buzz of power through my whole body, my greedy gaze taking him in, from his glazed-over eyes to his open mouth exposing his panting pink tongue to his compact, hard body. And his cock, stiff now and pointing straight to his chest as I pound into him.

"Feel good?" he asks with a cheeky smile, and I retaliate by snapping my hips hard, making us both groan.

"Yeah, it feels fucking good, you sexy little—" I bite back my words as I have to keep myself in check before I flood the condom too soon.

"Touch me," he says in a strained voice.

I shift the balance of my weight so I can wrap one hand around his cock, hot to the touch. I stroke him dry, flicking my thumb over the crown, damp at the slit.

I'm about to reach for the lube, but he digs his fingers into my hips. "Don't stop."

How can I ignore his request, especially when made with a throaty voice that goes straight to my balls? I keep up both rhythms, and when he starts spilling in my hand, I let myself go, too, the long-delayed orgasm so strong I think I pull a muscle with how hard I strain my neck as my climax shoots through me.

My hips stutter through the end, and I grab the base of the condom with one hand and my neck with the other as I pull out. "Shit."

"Yeah," Connor agrees, sounding dreamy.

I dump the condom into the trash, flop back on the bed. "No, I think I tweaked something."

"Oh no," he says, instantly switching from content to concerned. "Where?"

I point to my neck where the ache isn't going away.

"Turn over," he says, sounding businesslike.

I flop on my stomach, wincing at the sharp pain that results.

"Here?" he asks, pressing into the side of my neck.

"Lower—there." He kneads at the muscles, and magically the pain melts away. "Ahh. That's really helping."

He keeps it up, asks conversationally, "Was it good until you threw your beautiful neck out?"

"So good for me," I mumble into the pillow. "You?"

"So good for me, too," he whispers. He presses a kiss to the sore spot. "Go to sleep, angel. You'll feel better in the morning."

"You're staying, right?" I ask, half asleep already.

There's a pause. Longer than I was expecting. "I'm staying." The covers rustle as Connor slips underneath, settling into what's become his side of the bed. "I'm staying."

TWENTY-FIVE
CONNOR

THE WEEK PASSES SO QUICKLY it's Saturday again when I realize I've started to settle into a sort of routine. Last Saturday was errands, missing Shay while he was working in the flower shop, then game night at Melissa and Meadow's place, a cute rental near the elementary school. This time, both Jack and Pete joined us, making us three couples. It felt so good to be able to casually touch Shay, to flirt with him as much as I wanted. We went back to his place, of course, and in the morning I requested another cooking lesson, so Shay showed me how to make French toast, as promised, which is so freaking easy I'm embarrassed I didn't already know how to make it.

Sunday—the only day we both don't have work, though I am on call—we bundled up, packed a picnic and a thermos of tea, and drove to a nearby nature preserve for a wintry hike. The temps were above average and it was sunny and gorgeous when we got to our vantage point, where we could see down to a beautiful reservoir.

We ate our picnic in the special peace that being completely alone outdoors brings, then kissed in the sunlight, with nothing but the trees and the birds as our witnesses.

I've been riding high on those early relationship endorphins, everything buoyant and light because Shay exists. When we're together, it feels so good I finally understand what it means to be falling in love. Shay is someone who's literally changed my life just by being his incredible self. The walls of my old life have been tumbling down, one by one; my own preconceived notions, my fears, my doubts—they've all been crashing away like bricks smashed by a wrecking ball. Being with Shay is a simultaneous dismantling of the person I was before and a building up of the person I want to be.

Nothing can bring me down—except for the one big heavy brick I haven't managed to demolish.

I keep finding reasons not to talk to my parents. I've barely been home, for one thing, sequestered as I am on the weekends with my boyfriend, in his greenhouse of an apartment and magical, cozy bed. Then I've been putting in long hours at work. We've been busy with patients, of course, but I've also been working with Violet on updating some of our protocols and looking into new software to help her with the back-end tasks. Thankfully, Mom and Dad have been so busy with wedding preparations that they haven't commented on my absences.

And I continue to say nothing.

Every day I'm with Shay I know this is stupid and can't go on. But I've been so happy in our bubble—I'm selfish. I don't want anything to change.

I want to stay in Rosedale, keep working at the vet's office, keep being with Shay. But what if telling my mother I'm gay means my illusion of family and stability evaporates?

Worst-case scenario, I could try getting another job nearby. There seems to be enough work in the area.

But all of this is moot because right now I have to figure out what to wear to the bachelor party for my sister's fiancé tomorrow night. We're driving all the way to Bridgeport to go to a club, and instead of spending the last few weeks dreading it, I've just ignored it altogether.

Shit. Am I going to have to buy something? Jeans and a button down are the nicest things I have. But there's a clothing shop on Main Street—maybe I could find a nice sweater or blazer to dress everything up with.

I reluctantly left Shay this morning—he had work to do in the shop—but going back downtown gives me an excuse to drop by and visit.

> Have to come to town for an errand.
> Want me to pick up some lunch and
> bring it by the shop?

Then I wait, wondering if I'm being clingy, considering I only rolled out of his bed a couple of hours ago.

But he writes back a minute later.

> Lifesaver! Please! Turkey club!

> Actually, make that a hummus veggie.

I smile, wondering if he's skipping the meat on my behalf, which would be adorable, if unnecessary. I hit the clothing store first, where I gaze doubtfully at my wide array of options until an employee comes to my rescue.

"Can I help you?" a middle-aged man wearing a mustard sweater under a tweed blazer asks.

"Do you have anything I could wear to a bachelor party at a club that says, 'I'm happy you're marrying my sister but let's not get carried away tonight?'"

He chuckles and sizes me up. "Well, black is always classic and menacing if you want to send a message."

He pulls some items and half an hour later I'm leaving with new black jeans, a crisp white dress shirt, and a black blazer that actually fits me. I think I look pretty snazzy in the attire and can't help wondering what Shay will think. And then I feel terrible because it's another reminder that the wedding's in less than a week and all of my family will be there.

But Shay won't be. Because I suck.

I order sandwiches on autopilot from Ruth at Hot Brew and trudge over to the flower shop. I hate this roiling in my gut, this feeling that I'm not doing the right thing. Keeping this part of me separate from my family never bothered me before—or at least I never admitted that it bothered me before. But this can't go on.

I push open the flower shop door. Shay's with a customer, so I let myself around the back behind the counter and set the sandwiches out on Shay's worktable.

I poke around while I wait for him to finish. He's very organized, with all kinds of wraps and ribbons in labeled bins, tools all in their places. He's gotten out a bunch of clean, clear glass vases, and there's a note on top, *Courtney 2/14*, followed by a list of flowers.

He's getting the centerpieces ready for my sister's wedding, the wedding to which I am not taking him as my date.

Okay, maybe it's not crazy to not invite a guy I've only been seeing for a few weeks to a family wedding. I mean, that's understandable, right? But while it would be completely reasonable to exclude any of the other guys I've been with casually over the years, Shay's different. This is serious. And I'm not going to be able to keep him if I don't get serious, too.

Finally, he finishes with the customer, who departs happily with a large potted plant and a bag of gardening supplies. Shay drops onto the stool with a groan. "Busy morning."

"That's good, right?"

"That's always good in retail. Are you okay? You seem kind of preoccupied."

"I'm okay," I say, because it's not fair to unload on him when I'm the one with the problem. "I brought sandwiches."

He looks like he's going to say something else, but instead he lifts his hand to rub his neck.

"That still bothering you?" I move behind him, start kneading the tight spot he got when we were having sex last week.

"Ouch," he says when I hit the knot straight on.

This is my fault, too. "You should get a proper massage. Let me book one for you. There's a day spa in Midville. It's pricey, but worth it."

"You don't have to do that."

"I want to. God, Shay, you're so—"

"So what?"

There are so many ways I could end that sentence. So gorgeous. So kind. So hardworking. So sexy. So much what I want. But I don't feel like I have the right to shower him with praise, with the love that's building in my heart when I can't give him everything.

Instead, I press a kiss to the side of his neck. "I'm making you an appointment for Monday."

"God, I'd love to, sexy, but I'm going to be in the weeds all week filling orders for Valentine's."

"Oh, right." I know he's got a super busy week, culminating in the holiday—the same day as the wedding, which is at five p.m. at the Greystone Inn, one of the oldest buildings in Rosedale. It was converted from a fancy mansion to an equally fancy inn and event space a few years ago. "Then after Valentine's Day."

"That sounds so good. Thanks, Connor." He twists his upper body around to glance at me with his pretty, light eyes. They look blue today next to his denim work shirt. "Maybe we could make it a couple's massage."

"Yeah." I'd like to believe that after Valentine's Day I'll have my life sorted out and we could do such a normal couple-y thing. "Sounds great."

He smiles up at me and I'm lost for a second in those eyes that pull me in like twin tractor beams. But I don't lean in for the kiss I'm desperate for because the door to the shop opens, and we both instinctively look up to see who walks in. Like a slow-motion train wreck, I take in the fact that it's my mother and Violet, bundled against the cold, coming into the shop together. Mom's looking right at me, at my hands on Shay's shoulders, and like a chastened puppy, I drop my arms to my side quickly enough to damn me.

Mom glances at us with a puzzled look on her face, then her confusion seems to drain away, leaving a kind of eerie stillness. Violet bellies up to the counter, speaking first. "Connor, what the heck are you doing here?"

I don't look at Shay. I can't look at him. Here's my moment. "I brought Shay lunch," I say, my voice sounding far away to my own ears.

Violet looks back at her sister, but Mom doesn't say anything, though she walks closer to join her at the counter. "We came to ask if we can add a couple of things to the wedding order," Violet says.

There's one more excruciating second of silence and then Shay gets smoothly off the stool, shifts papers next to the register, and finds his trusty Moleskine notebook.

"Of course. What would you like to add?"

Violet nudges my mom. "Iris?"

"I don't think we met properly the other day," Mom says, offering Shay her hand. "I'm Iris."

"Shay Brierley," he says, shaking her hand firmly. I see her checking out the tattoos peeking out of his sleeve.

"It's always nice to meet a friend of Connor's."

That's it—that's my cue. All I have to do is say, "Actually Mom, Shay and I are dating." A few simple words and a decade-plus of lying by omission comes to an end.

But I can't.

"I'm Connor's Aunt Violet. I work next door, but I'm sad to say I haven't popped in here in a while. This place is remarkable. I didn't know Rodney was so interested in houseplants—or is this your doing?" my aunt adds shrewdly.

"I've made a few changes," Shay says modestly, seemingly oblivious to the awkward atmosphere. "I've been bringing in a lot more plants."

"Oh, look at these darling succulents," Violet says, touching a jade green petal on a nearby display.

"They are attractive," my mom agrees. "I've been meaning to get a gift for Mike's parents. Maybe they'd like one of these." She points to one of the large shallow ceramic dishes Shay potted up with a variety of intertwined succulents.

"Oh, that's perfect," Violet says.

"That dish was made by a local ceramicist who works out of the Rosedale Art Center. It's a one-of-a-kind piece," Shay explains.

What is happening right now? How are they shopping while I'm failing at the one thing that matters right now?

"And what did you want to add for the wedding?" Shay asks. "It's only that with Valentine's Day, we're tight on some of our supply."

"Oh, we wanted to get some small corsages for the little girls, my grandnieces. They're going to help out at the ceremony, so I thought it would be nice to give them something to feel official."

They talk details and I find enough mental bandwidth to admire Shay in his element, asking about sizes, flower types, and doing the math in his head when he quotes them the cost. But my emotions are currently rioting, turning over tables and knocking over chairs in my gut. My heart's beating so fast I have to order myself to take long calming breaths, the kind I coached myself to do when I would get underwater with studying for exams and needed a coping mechanism.

I'm slightly calmer by the time Shay and my mom finish their business. She's bought the big succulent arrangement for Mike's parents.

"One more thing—Connor, can you hand me those scissors?" Shay asks.

I snap out of my daze and hand him the big, heavy pair of fabric scissors. He cuts off a long piece of sage green ribbon and wraps it around the arrangement for a final flourish.

"You all set for the bachelor party?" Mom says to me while Shay's tying a jaunty bow.

"I think so," I answer, wondering if I sound normal. Doubtful.

Shay glances at me, but doesn't say anything. When I think they're leaving and my torture will be over, Violet decides she needs two aloes for her kitchen window, and I endure that transaction while avoiding my mother's stare.

Finally, *finally*, they're done.

"See you at home, Connor. And thank you, Shay," Mom says, lifting her gift with her good arm.

"Bye," I say faintly.

The door shuts behind them. I let out a breath, turn to Shay.

"You probably want me to leave now. So yeah. I'll go."

"Wait, why would I want you to go?" He puts a hand

out to stop me from retreating through the break in the counter to the front.

"I'm just—I'm so sorry." I squeeze my eyes shut in the vain hope it'll stop me from crying.

"Hey, what—what are you sorry about?"

"I didn't—I couldn't—I totally bunted, Shay. I could have told her right then that we're together. I could have just said the words instead of freezing, and I'm sorry."

"Are you sorry because you missed an opportunity, or are you sorry because you think I'm mad? Because you didn't do anything wrong."

"How can you say that? I stood there like a dolt and let you do all the heavy lifting." Now that they're gone, I can appreciate how gracefully Shay handled the situation. No thanks to me.

"Well, your mom was more relaxed than the last time she was in. And your aunt seems cool."

"I don't deserve you."

"Hey." Shay tugs on my arm again and we make eye contact, his expression grave. "Yes, you do," he says plainly and clearly. "You deserve to be yourself. You deserve to be happy." He licks his lips in what seems like a nervous gesture. "Does being with me make you happy?"

That's easy enough to answer. I have never been as happy as I am with Shay. But it's not fair of me to tell him when I'm what's holding us back. "Yes."

He looks faintly relieved at my response. "Then take all the time you need, okay? I'm not going anywhere."

Time. I've given myself too much of that, and this is where we ended up. I put my hand on Shay's arm. "Look,

I appreciate how patient you've been, but you're being way too easy on me."

He opens his mouth, and I can tell he's going to say something nice and supportive and it's going to make me feel even worse than I do now.

"No, just let me finish." He closes his mouth, and I go on, "I can't be with you, really be with you, until I resolve this with my family. You deserve that much, okay? So I'm going to go figure that out, and then I'll...get back to you."

He frowns. "It kind of sounds like you're breaking up with me."

I remember what he told me about his ex and the way he jerked Shay around, breaking things off, then declaring them back on again. "I'm not breaking up with you. But you said I could take time, right? The next time I see you, I want to be able to kiss you and not care who sees us. And you're right—I'm going to need a little more time."

"But—"

"Goodbye, Shay." I pick up my shopping bag, leave my sandwich. I've lost my appetite. I don't look back as I walk out the door.

TWENTY-SIX
SHAY

AS SOON AS Connor leaves the flower shop, a group of four young women comes in chatting and laughing amongst themselves, and I shift into sales mode, but my mind is racing, going over and over the events of the last half hour. I've lost my usual equilibrium that the plants and the shop bring me. Connor walked out of here, ostensibly to make things better, but I can't help but feel like I'm being punished for giving him the time he needs to figure things out.

The sting of him taking his hands off me the second his mom saw us pricks at my heart as well. It's not that I don't get it, but it still hurts as I go through the motions for the rest of the day.

But it hurts more that he's still not letting me fully into his life, and I've only got the vague assurance that we'll get there. I told him I wasn't going anywhere—but I'm not sure I can keep that promise.

I got the rejection call from the bank this morning. Unless I can put together substantially more than I have in the bank for a down payment, they can't loan me the amount I'd need to buy the building—something about my debt-to-income ratio. I'll have to consider my other options. One way or the other, it looks like I might have to start over.

As I tidy up the shop once I've locked the door for the evening, I glance at my workbench, at the preparations I've made for Courtney's wedding. I've got the busiest week of the year ahead of me. Normally I'd be excited and energized, but the joy has been sucked out by the double whammy of not getting the loan and Connor's abrupt departure. I'm doing the flowers for his sister's wedding, but the thought of being included as someone who's important to Connor is now just as much a pipe dream as becoming the owner of Rosedale Flowers and More.

Worst of all, I miss him.

MONDAY, I prep a bouquet for my mid-week wedding, then stay up late making sure the shop is spic and span and stocked up for the week ahead. I'm almost out of Valentine's Day-specific greeting cards, and I make a note to order more for next Valentine's Day.

If I'm even in business this time next year.

While I work, I think about contingency plans. I could ask Rodney if he'll consider selling me the flower shop alone. But if that's a no-go, I can take my savings and try to open up a shop of my own. Rosedale retail space isn't impossible to come by. I could start fresh—do everything my way from the start. It would mean a lot of hard work for months—maybe even years—to get things profitable. But I don't mind hard work.

I'd have to move, of course. I wouldn't hate saying goodbye to my too-small apartment, but I'd probably end up in another economical rental. The idea of buying my own house, putting in a garden and a greenhouse—it all seems so laughably impossible.

And not that I'm ready to admit defeat, but not having Connor around this week, plus the temperature dropping to its coldest point all winter, reminds me that I miss my family. I even miss Arizona. I suppose I can always move back, get a job at a plant shop there. Get on the dating apps. Avoid Ben.

Ugh.

But then I remind myself I was doing fine in Rosedale—better than fine—before Connor came into my life. And if he suddenly—my heart pangs at the thought, but I make myself consider the possibility—went out of it, I'd do fine again. I'd simply have to wait for another handsome, cute, smart guy with a steady job to walk through my door and flirt with me about baked goods.

Happens all the time.

IT'S the day before Valentine's Day and I'm going to do my job of bringing happiness and romance to people on this artificial-but-good-for-business holiday, even if I'm not exactly feeling the romance myself.

There's a rush right after I open, people picking up

all sorts of things, from preordered arrangements and bouquets to potted plants. I even sell two pairs of the gold monstera earrings I ordered on a whim even though I never stocked jewelry before. Monstera plants, with their big glossy leaves with Swiss-cheese style holes, are perennial favorites, and jewelry based on their design seems to be just as popular.

Tomorrow's the wedding, and I haven't heard from Connor all week. I'm worried about him, to be honest. He wasn't in the best place the last time I saw him, and he's probably spent more time with his family this week than usual. I hope he's okay. I've texted him a couple of times, just to say hi, and all I got back was a thumbs-up.

I'm too busy to seriously consider whether that thumbs-up is a symbol that I'm being dumped. And then someone walks through my door—almost the last person I ever expected to see come into the flower shop.

"Tye? What the—" My brother walks in, broad smile on his face. He's an inch shorter than me, but shares our dad's lanky build. His hair is as light as mine, cut short. He's wearing the biggest puffy coat I've ever seen.

I'm waiting on a regular customer, so I introduce them—"Mrs. Kaufman, this is my brother"—before coming around the counter to give him a big hug to match his big coat.

"Oh, how nice," Mrs. Kaufman says, giving us a smile.

"What are you doing here? Is everything okay?" Before he can answer, the door opens again and my mom and dad walk through, dressed for the chilly weather in slightly less ostentatious outerwear. "What the fuck?"

"Language, Blueberry," my mom chides, then she smiles and pulls me in for a hug. My mother is a five-foot-tall woman married to a six-three Swedish guy with two over six-foot kids. Our family portraits are hilarious.

"Hey, kiddo," my dad says, taking his turn in the hug line.

"Hi, Dad. I'm so confused right now."

"Well, I mentioned that we wanted to come visit," Mom says as if it's obvious why they're here. "And you said to come anytime."

"Anytime except this exact moment." I remember the conversation clearly even though it was weeks ago, B.C. Before Connor. "I'm slammed with Valentine's Day."

"Yes, you did say that, but we were able to get good flights and I rented the most darling house for a whole week—the bed-and-breakfast didn't work out—so we figured we'd come and surprise you. We flew in last night and we had breakfast at this great coffee shop—"

I cut her off before she can tell me their individual orders. "Well, I'm surprised." I glance at Mrs. Kaufman, waiting semi-patiently by the register. "Um, look around, I guess. I need to finish with my customer."

"Of course, son," Dad booms. "The customer always comes first." He and Mom poke around the houseplants and Tye takes off his coat.

"They made me promise not to tell you," Tye says.

"Is Jen here, too?"

"No, she had to work. But we have some news."

Mrs. Kaufman clears her throat.

Tye nods at the register. "I'll tell you later."

I ring Mrs. Kaufman up, then sell another pair of

monstera earrings to a man grateful to find a unique gift for his wife, then get a phone order for a bouquet for tomorrow. The cutoff for pre-orders was days ago, but I take pity when they beg me to do it, especially after they quickly agree to pay the large rush fee I tack on.

"You *are* busy," Mom says. She's taken off her ski jacket and looks great in a white sweater and her signature silver and turquoise jewelry. "Can we help?"

"What? You want to help?"

"You know I used to work retail," she says. "I was in the furniture department at Macy's when I met your father."

"How could I forget?" I've heard the story of their meet-cute a million times. Dad was shopping for a couch for his bachelor pad and made her show him every single model just so he could keep talking to her. By the end of the day, Mom made a big commission selling him the biggest, most expensive couch in the store, and Dad had Mom's phone number.

"Put us to work," Dad says. "We came here to check out your—"

My brother elbows him in the side, and I don't have time to wonder what that's about because the phone rings again.

This entire thing is a little wacky, but I'm not going to turn down free labor. "Okay, Mom, can you answer the phone? Tye, you could actually take this order down the street to the dentist's office. The address is on the tag. You can map it, but it's literally one block to the left, one block to the right. Dad, how are you with point of sale?

You can work the register while I put together a bouquet."

My father literally rolls up the sleeves of his plaid dress shirt. "What system are you on?"

I tell him, and he rubs his hands together. "Perfect. That's what we use at all fourteen Burger Buster locations."

And suddenly my family members are my temporary employees, and I have an actual moment to look at my phone and see that I have no new messages from Connor.

No big deal. I have a business to run.

And I can run it, even if my heart's a little sore.

IT'S my sister's wedding day and I feel terrible. I haven't seen Shay since I walked out of his shop Saturday, and every day we've been apart, my heartache has gotten worse. I fiddle with my boutonniere. One of the flower shop's occasional helpers delivered it to the house this morning. Touching it, my fingers feel warm—Shay made this with his two clever hands.

I promised him I'd fix this, and I haven't. I left the shop almost a week ago determined to man up and talk to my parents, but when I arrived home, Mike's parents were there. I'd forgotten they were staying in the other guest room for the weekend until their rental was available on Monday. I suffered through dinner with them and my parents, my mom giving me odd looks, but there was no opening to have the big talk. Sunday, they were all gone by the time I got up. Then the bachelor party was that night—it wasn't a debacle, but I didn't exactly have the best time. I stayed sober and reined in Mike's cousin Binky, who at one point tried to talk everyone into driving to Atlantic City, and when that didn't go over, to Manhattan to go clubbing. Luckily, cooler heads prevailed. Mike seemed to have a good time, and no one went to jail, which meant I fulfilled my mandate.

The workweek felt busier than ever since we were packing in as many appointments as we could in order to close on Friday for the wedding. I ended every day completely wrung out, but maybe that was because my self-imposed isolation from Shay was draining me as much as work was. Violet commented on it on Thursday night when we were cleaning up. "You need to get some sleep, Connor. Big day tomorrow."

It has been a big day already. Courtney and Mike opted to skip a traditional rehearsal dinner, so this morning we were all at the Greystone Inn for a run-through of the ceremony, and then we came back to my parents' house, which is ground zero for the bride's side of the wedding party to get dressed and coiffed. I put on my wedding suit an hour ago and now I'm pacing in the living room, trying to stay out of the way. I keep thinking about Shay, about how today is even busier for him. I'm such a jackass. Not for the first time this week, I think that he's better off without me.

I should just break things off and save him the trouble of being with someone like me—someone who can't communicate the simplest facts about himself to the people who matter the most.

I finger my cell phone in my pocket, but even I'm not a big enough coward to break up with him by text or via a phone call.

Plus, there's the fact that I don't want to break up with him at all.

"Oh, there you are," Violet says, sticking her head around the living room door. "Have you seen the corsages for the little girls? They aren't with the other flowers."

"No, but I'm sure they're somewhere. Shay wouldn't forget." I swallow hard, his name painful in my mouth.

"No, I suppose he wouldn't." She pauses, then comes fully into the room. She's wearing a flattering A-line burgundy dress that adheres to my sister's color palette for the extended family. "Why isn't he coming to the wedding, Connor? I asked your sister, and she said you hadn't invited him."

"What? Why would I invite him?" I say, feeling nauseous.

"Connor." She takes a deep breath. "You're obviously involved with him. Unless something happened since last weekend. You've been down—something did happen, didn't it?"

She knows. She knows, and she didn't say anything. Typical. "Nothing happened," I say, forcing the words out around the growing lump in my throat. "And I can't believe you're bringing this up *now*. The wedding is in an hour."

"Well, I would have brought it up sooner, but you're always so...closed off about this stuff."

"Closed off? *I'm* closed off?" I'm aware that my voice is rising, but I can't seem to help it. "Where do you think I learned that?" I ask bitterly.

"Violet, I found the corsages," Mom says, joining us in her own wine-colored gown. Her cast has been wrapped in a matching scarf for the occasion. "Oh Connor, you're here, too. Good. It's been such a busy week, but I've been wanting to mention this. Violet and I would love to have you join the practice permanently. We can have papers drawn up this week outlining the role, remuneration—"

"Stop. Please, just stop talking."

"What? Why?" She blinks as if she wasn't expecting to be contradicted.

"Because I have to tell you something." I look at my mother's face, lightly made up for the wedding and icily beautiful. She's offering me a future in Rosedale, and I can't let myself take it until I actually show her my real self. "I know you don't like talking about feelings. I know my emotions have always seemed like an inconvenience to you, but I have to say a few things because if I don't, I'm afraid this part of me will die and I'll never get it back."

Mom just looks at me like she has no idea what I'm talking about. But I plow on. If I don't do this now, I know I never will.

"All I wanted when I was growing up was to be like you, Mom. At work, I saw you be so caring, so reassuring. I wanted to do what you did. I wanted to help people the way you did. I wanted to make you proud. Joining the practice would have made my ten-year-old self so happy."

"That's why you became a vet? Because you wanted to be...like me?" She sounds flabbergasted.

"Yeah," I admit. "And I think I wanted you to notice me."

"What is that supposed to mean?"

"It means you never seemed to care about anything except when I got A's, or my team was winning in baseball, or I had a date to the prom. You didn't want to hear it when I struggled in some of my classes to get those A's, that I hated baseball, that I asked a girl to the prom, even though—" I stop, breathe. I can do this.

"Even though?" she asks with raised eyebrows.

"Even though I'm gay," I say. Whisper, really. But she heard me. I can tell by her sharp intake of breath and the way her features relax into that mask of stillness I saw in Shay's shop the other day.

Violet moves toward me, and it feels like backup. I appreciate the gesture.

"So that's—" She swallows hard. "I didn't know."

"I know."

She looks at Violet, who's gazing at me with a proud smile on her face.

"But I sort of did? You never mentioned girls in Chicago. I figured you were just focused on school."

"I was focused on school. But there were never any girls to mention, Mom."

"The other day—in the flower shop…"

"Shay and I have been seeing each other." I want to tell her he's my boyfriend, but I'm not sure I'm allowed to anymore after offering him nothing but radio silence all week.

I see her struggle with what to say. I give her time, because that's all I can do right now.

"I know I'm not the warmest and fuzziest mom," she says finally, surprising me. "But I do love you. You know that, right?" She looks at me as if she isn't sure what she'll do if I don't say yes.

So I tell her the truth. "I know." Her shoulders drop in relief. "But it's nice to hear it, Mom."

"I'm sorry if you felt you couldn't tell me before. Or I'm sorry for not...asking?" She's uncertain, but she's trying.

"I didn't tell you because I didn't want you to see me differently, but it turns out I kept you from seeing who I really am. And I can't not be who I am anymore."

"Good," she says simply. As if it is that simple. And maybe it is, on some level.

"So, can I mention this to your father?"

I let out a startled laugh. She's talking about it like I got a bad grade in physics. "I can tell him."

"Tell me what?" Dad says, choosing that moment to come in, his dark red necktie hanging loose around his neck.

"I'm gay, Dad," I say, finding the words faster with Mom and Violet looking at me encouragingly.

"Oh." He blinks, his processing expression on his face. "That actually makes a lot of sense."

"Does it?"

He pats me awkwardly on the back. "Good for you."

"Thanks." I guess my parents get points for trying, but they'll never be warm and fuzzy, as Mom put it.

"Can you do my tie? I'm all thumbs today," Dad says. He turns to Mom, then stops. "Never mind. I forgot about your arm."

"I can't wait to get this blasted thing off," Mom says, tugging at the scarf around her cast.

"I can do it," Violet says, stepping up to my father, who's shuffling his feet back and forth. "Oh, Art, stand still. Your daughter is getting married. It's normal to be a little nervous."

Mom looks at the clock on the mantel. "Speaking of Courtney, she's got to take her curlers out. We leave for the venue in half an hour."

"I'll find her," I say, seizing on the opportunity to escape the room. Like a delayed reaction, my cheeks grow hot as I scale the stairs in search of my sister. I told them. Well, Violet had drawn her own conclusion. But Mom and Dad. They know. And maybe not everything is resolved—I didn't hear Mom asking me to join the practice *after* I told her I'm gay—but it's out there. I feel like I can breathe for the first time since I left Shay in the flower shop a week ago.

Courtney isn't in the guest room where she's been getting ready. She's not in any of the other bedrooms, either, but then I hear water running in the bathroom at the end of the hall. I knock on the door. "Courtney? You in there?"

"Connor?"

"Yep."

She cracks the door open. She's got curlers in her hair and is wearing a white bathrobe and she looks as pale as the terrycloth despite her full face of makeup.

"I threw up," she says, sounding miserable.

"Oh shit. Are you sick?" I take an instinctive step back. I do not want to catch a stomach bug.

"I think—I think I'm pregnant."

I blink at her. I might have dad's processing face on.

Then I snap out of it. "Well, that puts me just coming out to Mom and Dad in perspective."

"You did? Oh, that's great, Connor." She puts a hand on her stomach, then brings it to her mouth. "I'm so nauseous. What do I do?"

"If it's pregnancy, it's the hormones. I'll bring you some saltines. It's better to keep something in your stomach. How many weeks do you think you are?"

"Weeks? How should I know? Who measures things in weeks?"

"Pregnant people, for some reason," I say. "Do you want me to call Mike?"

"I guess so. I mean, what if I'm not? I sort of thought maybe I was showing signs, but I was so busy with the wedding that I just put it out of my head. Like if I didn't think about it, it wouldn't be real."

I sadly know exactly what she's talking about.

"But I guess I should find out. Take a test. I mean, Mike should know, right?"

"I think he'd marry you either way, if that's what you're asking."

She smacks my arm. "I know he'd marry me, that's not what I meant. I mean—"

"What's going on, you two? You need to take your curlers out," Mom says, coming up behind me.

"Oh god." Courtney sinks to the ground and puts her head in her hands.

I crouch down and speak in a soothing tone. "I'm going to call Mike, then I'm getting you some crackers, then I'll get someone to get us a test. You take out your curlers, okay?"

"Okay," she croaks. "Thanks Connor."

"What the hell is happening?" Mom asks.

"I might be pregnant," Courtney says, sounding tired. "And I need to throw up again." She scoots back and shuts the door in our faces.

I grin at my Mom. "Well, Courtney did say she wanted her wedding day to be unforgettable."

"AND THAT IS the final delivery of the day," I declare as Tye and I climb into the florist van for the quick drive back to the shop. I was able to leave Mom and Dad in charge for half an hour while Tye and I brought a big Valentine's Day order to the assisted living facility.

Having my family here the last two days has been equal parts helpful and crazy-making. Case in point, my brother, who keeps asking questions about Connor that I can't answer. I evaded the topic of my absent boyfriend last night over dinner with my family at Nina's, the Italian place on Main Street, while Tye told us the joyous news that Jen was three months pregnant.

"How can she be three months pregnant when you weren't even sure you wanted to be a dad like a month ago?" I asked.

"Yeah, so it turns out the reason she'd been in such a bad mood with me was because she'd realized she was pregnant, but I'd been such a pill about it she wasn't sure she wanted to raise a kid with me." He winces, knowing how that makes him sound. "But we talked, and we straightened it all out. And I'm going to be the best father I can be," he said, sounding scared and proud at the same time.

"Yeah, you will," I said, proud of him, too. "Sometimes couples aren't always on the same page, but that's okay. They figure it out."

"Oh, yeah?" He looked like he wanted to turn the tables on me, but luckily our meals arrived, and I was able to avoid getting into it about Connor. Until now.

"So, just making sure I have this straight," he says to me as I negotiate the late-afternoon traffic, such as it is. "Connor wasn't out to his parents, and you told him you'd give him all the time he needed, and then he ghosted you to go to a bachelor party and a wedding that you did the flowers for and aren't invited to?"

"Well, I don't know if I'd call it ghosted," I say, defensive on Connor's behalf. "Look, it's complicated. I'm not making him coming out to his parents a condition of our being together."

"That's because you're a good guy, Shady," Tye says. "But good guys get taken advantage of."

"Connor's not taking advantage of me," I protest. "He's just on a different timeline. Remember how sometimes couples aren't always on the same page?" I ask tartly.

"Point taken." Tye nods. "But I just don't want you to get invested in someone who's not invested in you back." Like Ben, is the unspoken implication.

"Look, I appreciate the concern. I do. And I appreciate the help. But you need to let me live my own life, Tye Dye."

We park behind the shop and get out. I've got to touch base with my parents, triple check I filled all the day's orders, and clean up the shop before I can go home and sleep for a week, or at least twelve hours. I already posted to social media that I'd be opening the shop late tomorrow to give myself a much-needed break.

"Oh, Shay, so glad you're here," Mom says when we let ourselves into the back of the shop. "You are officially sold out of roses. And I got someone to buy the last of those adorable monstera earrings."

Dad's helping a customer choose a planter from the pottery shelf, so I take a moment to check on the day's totals. I blink when I see the numbers. This is the best day the shop has ever had, and it doesn't even take into account the weddings. "Great job, Mom, thanks."

A few minutes later, we've rung up that final customer. I gladly switch the sign on the door to closed, then lock up. "We did it," I say, collapsing onto a stool. "We survived Valentine's Day."

"I think this calls for a toast," my dad says, producing a bottle of sparkling wine from the flower fridge.

"Where did that come from?"

"That wine shop a few blocks away. I even have glasses, sort of," he says, pulling four paper cups from under the counter. He pops the bottle and serves us in turn. I take my cup and look at it glumly, wishing I felt more like celebrating. What's Connor doing right now? Toasting to his sister's marriage with the rest of his family?

It could be worse. At least I'm not alone right now. Not for the first time since they got here, I experience a wave of gratitude that my family decided to crash into my life practically uninvited. I know it's because they care.

"Kiddo, your mother and I want to tell you how proud we are of you," Dad says with the air of someone about to make a speech. I take a tentative sip of the bubbly—which is quite tasty, actually.

"Thanks, guys," I say genuinely.

"You've worked so hard, and you have made this shop a true success," he goes on. "Now, a little bird told us that you might lose this place when the owner sells the property."

I glare at my brother, who stares innocently into his cup.

"And we wanted to tell you that we have a proposition for you."

"What's that?" I take a large sip of wine.

"What if we gave you the seed money to open your own shop? Flower shop, plant shop, whatever, all yours. We'd help with whatever you need to get it going."

"Oh my god." I can't believe they would do that for me. My mind races ahead with ideas and next steps. What about locations? Maybe on the street that the library's on, it gets decent foot traffic and—

"We could help you find the perfect spot in Scottsdale," Dad says. "There's a new mall opening next year that might be a good fit. That gives us time to do market research, and—"

"Wait. You'd give me money to open my own shop. But it has to be in Arizona?"

"Well, yes, Blueberry," Mom says, as if that's obvious. "You've shown us you can make it work here, but in Scottsdale we can leverage our network, get you the best rates on things. Dad could use you for all of his client gifts. Think about the possibilities. You could end up with a mini chain of your own. Shay's Flowers and More." She pauses. "Okay, we'll workshop the name, but you get the idea."

I stand up and set my cup down on the counter. The wine suddenly tastes sour. "I get the idea all right. You want to help me out. But only on your terms. I thought by coming here and getting to see this town, and the shop, you'd see how happy I am here. You'd see that this is the life I want. I want you to be proud of me. I want you to be a part of my life, but I want that life to be here."

My mom looks at me like she's about to cry, and my dad frowns at his drink.

Tye is the only one who says anything. "You have a great life here—no one's saying you don't. But we miss you. And what does Rosedale have that Scottsdale doesn't? I mean, they both have dale in the name."

I don't bother smiling at the terrible joke. "I don't hate Scottsdale. But I live here now. And I'm not coming back. I need you guys to respect that. I love you. But I came here to prove to myself I could make it on my own and I've done that. Is it perfect? Clearly not. But it's what I want. And I had a feeling you wouldn't understand, which is why I didn't tell you that I had a chance to buy the business, to buy the entire building, in fact, and really invest in my future, but it didn't work out. I don't have enough cash for a down payment. I didn't want to ask you for help because I knew you'd say no. Well, I might have to start over, as you so sensitively noted, but if I do, it's going to be here. In Rosedale. My home. Can you try to understand? Please?"

My dad looks at my mom, who looks at me, her eyes wet. "We'll try, Blueberry—but—"

"No buts," I say, exasperated. The phone in the shop rings shrilly. It's after hours, but I lean over the counter and snatch up the receiver, anyway.

"What?" I bark into the phone. I listen to the voice on the other end and my jaw drops. "What?" I ask again. I'm having trouble processing what I'm hearing, and it's not because of a few sips of bubbly. "I'm not sure I can—" The customer interrupts me, and I find myself agreeing. "Okay. I'll be there."

"What is it?" Tye asks, concerned.

"You guys better go to dinner without me. We can talk about this more later. If there's anything else to talk about."

"What—why?" he asks.

"I have one more delivery to make."

I TROT DOWNSTAIRS, call Mike, and tell him to leave the venue and come over to the house. "It's nothing bad," I say, "but Courtney really needs to see you."

"You're scaring me, man," he says.

"Seriously, it's okay. Oh, and I'm gay," I add, while I'm on a roll.

"Okay?" He sounds less than thrilled, but I hang up so he can concentrate on getting over here.

Then I make another call while I look for crackers in the pantry, but Shay's cell goes straight to voicemail. Of course. It's his busy day.

"Damn." Who else can I call? The bridesmaids have already departed for the venue, and I don't have any of their phone numbers. I might have to make a run to the drugstore myself. But then I remember one other person in town I can try.

"Melissa? It's Connor. Are you working? If so, just tell me and I'll ask someone else."

"I actually just got off my shift. Why?"

"I can't really explain right now, but can you do me a huge favor and go to the drugstore and get me a pregnancy test? I'll text you my address and I'll pay you back."

There's a moment of silence. "I never thought I'd be getting that particular request from you, but sure. What the hell."

"Thank you so much." I text her our address and try Shay once more. Voicemail. I could call him at the store, but I don't want to be an asshole and interrupt what he's doing just because it suits my schedule. Instead, I bring the crackers to Courtney, who munches on one delicately. "Where's Mom?" I ask.

"She's calling the venue to push everything back by an hour."

"Smart. Mike's on his way, as is a pregnancy test. I tried not to scare the shit out of him, but I'm not sure how good a job I did."

"Okay, thanks. God, this is so embarrassing."

"Why? You guys want kids, right?"

"In like three to five years. That was the plan." I stare at her until she throws a cracker at me. "I know, I know, life doesn't always go according to plan," she grumbles.

"Tell me about it."

"I'm glad you told Mom and Dad. How were they?"

"Dad was Dad. Mom was...surprisingly emotional. Violet being there helped. She pretty much already knew. I think it's going to be okay."

"Good for you."

"Yeah. I don't know." I'm still shaky from the adrenaline of having actually done it, and I don't feel particularly proud of myself. "I should have said it a long time ago."

"Whatever. They know now." She crunches another cracker. "This is helping, thanks." She smiles at me weakly and I smile back, glad to share this moment with my baby sister.

A moment later, I hear thundering feet on the stairs. "Your fiancé is here, Courtney." I get up to go meet Mike.

"Where is she?" Mike practically yells as he stomps toward me.

"In here, big guy," I say, pointing to the bathroom.

He races to her. "Baby, what's going on?"

I sidle away, letting them have privacy. The knock on the front door gives me purpose—I rush downstairs and open it to find Melissa, her brown curls stuffed under a red knitted cap. She thrusts a paper bag in my face. "I'm going to need payment in the form of information."

"It's for my sister," I explain. "And thank you."

"Anytime. You look dressed up. Oh my god, today's the wedding. Oh my god." Her mouth falls open as she puts it all together. "Well, congratulations."

"I'll fill you in on everything later. Thank you so much, again."

"What are friends for?" She says it so easily, but it means a lot to me to have friends in Rosedale who I can rely on for things both as zany as this and as simple as a cup of tea.

"Everyone's having so much family drama this week. You with the wedding and the—" She waves at the paper bag. "—Shay, with his family. Meadow's brother broke his leg snowboarding. Must be something in the air."

"Too bad about Meadow's brother," I say, vaguely recalling she has a brother a couple of years younger than us. "But what's that about Shay's family?"

"How his whole family just showed up out of the blue from Arizona. Apparently, he put them to work in the shop because he's so swamped with V-day. I would have thought he'd have told you."

He probably would have if I weren't avoiding him. "Well, I've been distracted with wedding stuff. And I'm a jerk."

"No, you're not," she says, scolding me. "But now I better go. Meadow and I are going to Sparkle. Cosmos are half-price all Valentine's Day."

"Have fun." She leaves, and I take the stairs two at a time to toss the bag to my sister, who has more color in her cheeks now. Mike's smiling ear to ear, so I guess the news that they might be deviating from their plan isn't coming as much of a blow.

"Thanks. I guess everything's going ahead, as long as I don't barf my way down the aisle."

"Keep eating," I advise. "I'll tell Mom and Dad we're good to go."

Fifteen minutes later, the pregnancy test affirms my sister's suspicions. I'm going to be an uncle.

Fifteen minutes after that, Courtney's got her curlers out and looks, if not radiant, then perfectly put together in her wedding finery—an old-fashioned, long-sleeved, ivory drop-waisted dress. Mike's grin has only gotten wider, if that's possible. We were originally supposed to go over in one car, but since Mike has a vehicle here, he takes Dad and Violet while I drive with Mom in the front and Courtney in the back—her dress spread out over the upholstery. Mom and Courtney do the math on the drive, and they figure out she's maybe six weeks along.

"Am I going to have to tell everyone that's why we're running late?" she asks.

"No, we'll just say there was a curler emergency," Mom says.

I laugh. "Why don't we blame it on the practice? We got a last-minute call and had to take care of it."

"We?" Mom looks at me with arched brows.

"Yeah." We stop at a light and I stare at her evenly, remembering what Violet said about asking for what I want. "It is our practice, right?"

"It will be, after we work out a contract," she says pointedly.

I laugh. That sounds like her. "Can't wait, Mom."

Everything's not perfect. My family is bonkers, but I'm beginning to appreciate that about them. The only problem is that Shay's not there. I bite my tongue and do my part, getting us to the venue safely. There's a bit of a commotion as we arrive, Violet helping Courtney out of the car and up the series of wide stone steps that lead to the entrance to the Greystone Inn, but then everyone settles down for the main event.

It's a beautiful ceremony. I allow myself to shed more than my share of tears. But for once, I don't care. My family can just deal with the fact that I cry sometimes.

As soon as the newly minted husband and wife kiss, I wonder if it's possible for me to slip out and go visit Shay. It's awful timing, but I have to tell him that I'm not going to let anything stop me from being with him anymore, not even myself.

But I get swept along on the tide of wedding rituals. Endless aunts and uncles and cousins all want to say hello. Then someone pushes champagne into my hand, and the photographer herds us to take a million pictures. Dinner's about to be served, and that's when I realize I am starving.

I drop into my chair at the table I've been painstakingly assigned near the main wedding party, and my gaze falls on the centerpiece. It's a charming low arrangement of red and cream roses, broken up by lush green leaves. It's wintery and romantic at the same time, and it makes my heart ache for the man who made it. I check my phone. The shop has been closed for a while. It's Valentine's Day. And I'm at a wedding without my gorgeous boyfriend. Clearly, I've made some bad decisions in my life.

"One more wedding-related request, Connor," Courtney says, bouncing up to my table, her usual energy seemingly restored. "I have a late delivery coming to the front—can you sign for it?"

"A delivery of what?" I ask as I push back from the table, but she's gone already. I look longingly at the buffet, then head to the front entrance. Just as I get there, someone walks through the front door, holding a paper-wrapped bouquet. It's my someone.

It's Shay.

"Oh my god, you're here."

He gives me a grimace-like smile. He looks tired, but he's a balm for my sore heart in his familiar coat and scarf. "Your mom called the shop and basically demanded I personally deliver a bouquet of dahlias here. Something about an unexpected wedding guest."

"My *mom* called you? And made you come here?"

"Is everything okay? I saw you called a couple of times earlier, but I couldn't answer."

"Everything is...weird. Oh my god, I have so much to tell you." I step close. "I am so, so glad you're here. Can you stay for a little while? Or maybe a long while?" I ask, echoing what he asked me the first night we spent together.

His smile is heartbreakingly hesitant. "Are you sure that's a good idea?"

I push up on my toes and kiss him, not caring who sees. "Yes."

But Shay takes a resolute step back from me. "I don't know, Connor. I think I should go."

He pushes the flowers at me, avoiding my gaze, and turns, leaving the way he came in.

THIRTY
SHAY

I'M at the top of the wide steps of the Greystone Inn, a place I've only been to deliver flowers, contemplating the van parked in the inn's visitor spot. It started to snow on the way over here, lazy oversized flakes that aren't going to amount to much, but made my drive silently beautiful, like traveling through an oil painting.

Why did I leave? The stress and pain of the last week, of having to go through the days without Connor in my life, caught up with me and I got spooked. I've put my heart on the line over and over for him and I'm too worn down to do it again tonight, of all nights.

I'm halfway down the series of stone steps when the door opens behind me.

"Wait, Shay." Connor sounds worried and I immediately want to fold him into a hug and tell him everything's going to be okay, but I can't when I don't know that. Still, I turn around and look up at him, all classy in his gray suit and dark red tie. "Please don't go," he says. "Can't you come in, even for a second?"

"It's been a really long day," I say. "I've been on my feet for ten hours."

"I know. You're amazing." He looks back through the open door, still holding the flowers I made him take. "Come in and sit down, then. Have something to eat. The food is really good, from what I hear. I bet you're starving."

Food does sound pretty tempting. My parents and brother went to dinner without me when I scrambled to fill Iris Nieves's strange request.

But as much as I want to go to the reception with Connor, I can't do it as his friend.

"I don't think I can, Connor," I say carefully. "It's not —it's not fair. It's not good for me, anyway. This week has been really hard." It hurts to be so honest when all I want is to be with him—common sense be damned.

His face falls, and I imagine the soles of my boots are glued to the stone steps so I don't march back up them.

"I get it—I do," he says, walking down until we're on the same step, our height difference restored. "Listen, I know I've been horrible, no matter how many times you say I'm not. I haven't been...true. To myself, mainly. And I obviously ended up hurting you, too. But Shay, you have astonished me in every way since the moment we met and all I can say is I'm a lucky bastard for having gotten to know you. And while that doesn't make up for the fact that I couldn't be what you deserved, I wanted to tell you." He gulps in air and when he exhales, I can see his breath. He looks at me, steady, his brown eyes intent on me. "I think I'm in love with you. And if you'd give me another chance—"

"Yes." The word's out of my mouth before I know what I'm doing.

"Yes, what?"

"Yes, I'll give you a chance. I'll give you all the chances. I think I love you, too." Love makes sense—it's the only thing that explains why I'm willing to face a roomful of his relatives on the slimmest of promises.

"I told my parents. Everything. It was a bit of a bombshell, but we all survived."

I give in to my instincts and gather him against my chest, his suit jacket cold to my touch, his hair damp from the falling snow where I press my cheek against it. The paper around the bouquet of flowers crinkles where it's smashed between us. "Oh, wow, Connor. That's huge."

"Yeah. But then Courtney found out she's pregnant, so that was another bombshell. It's been a day for bombshells."

His sister's pregnant? I didn't see that coming.

"And I'm freezing and I think you should come in and meet my family, for real." He shivers in my arms and pulls back to look at me. I gaze at the face I've been longing for, at the man offering me everything I want.

"There's more to say, but for now, would you come in and have some dinner and let me show you off?" He looks so earnestly hopeful—who am I to tell him no?

"I'm not dressed for a wedding," I say halfheartedly.

"You always look incredible," he returns easily. His free hand slips into mine and he pulls me up the steps and into the lobby, where it's about forty degrees warmer. "Let me take your coat. Wait—" He sets the bouquet down on a bench, then takes my coat and scarf. He disappears around a corner and comes back without them. "Coat room," he explains briefly. "Now, you want to use the bathroom or anything?"

I smooth down the front of my vest, the one I wore for our ill-fated date at the Art Center. I push my hair behind my ears and adjust my rings. Shoulders straight, I smile at him. "I'm ready."

He takes my hand, kisses the knuckles, and grins at me. My heart turns over. He's my brave, beautiful boyfriend. And he loves me. He thinks.

"Oh, the flowers." He picks them up, then sticks his nose in the opening of the paper, even though these dahlias don't have a scent. "They're beautiful. But I should be the one giving you flowers today."

"Why don't we share them?" I ask, feeling dazed.

"Deal."

No one seems to notice when we go into the Greystone Inn's main event room, busy as they are consuming dinner. Connor deposits our flowers at what I assume is his assigned seat, then we head to the buffet and get in line behind a middle-aged woman who Connor introduces to me as his cousin Robin. "Robin, this is my boyfriend, Shay."

"Oh!" She glances at our still-joined hands, gives us a broad smile. "I didn't know you were...in a relationship, Connor. Nice to meet you, Shay."

"Nice to meet you." We chat for a few minutes—the type of meaningless small talk you make at weddings. I try to keep up my end of the conversation even though I missed the ceremony and the only person I really know here is Connor. He seems pretty calm, even when another guest does a pointed double take when he sees us standing hip to hip.

I honestly feel like I'm in some sort of parallel universe, not sure how well I'm doing at being the boyfriend in this scenario. For three years, I wanted to have this sort of relationship with Ben, but he never let me in. And since I landed in Rosedale, I've been used to flying solo and being content with that. I'm not particularly experienced in this sort of couple's event. But I think I could learn to like it.

When it's our turn to get food, I squeeze Connor's hand. "You're going to have to let go, I think."

He slowly releases me. "Is this okay?" he asks under his breath as we get plates and fill them with delicious-looking Moroccan food, which is apparently a favorite of the bride and groom.

"So far, so good. Are you okay?"

"I'm sweating bullets," he says. "But I'm good." His smile is strong, and I couldn't be prouder of him.

We make our way to our table, which seems to be made up of second-tier wedding party members, and everyone greets us pleasantly enough. The food is fantastic. Connor leaves the table briefly to get us glasses of wine from the open bar. The DJ is playing eighties hits. I begin to relax, feeling less out of place when I start chatting with the date of one of the bridesmaids, David, who's into horticulture.

We're deep in conversation about orchids when Connor's sister approaches the table. She gives me a big hug, startling both myself and Connor, but I accept it graciously. "Congratulations, Courtney."

"Thanks. It's been a wild day. I'm sure Connor will tell you all about it if he hasn't already. I wanted to say thank you for the gorgeous flowers again."

"You did these arrangements? They're exceptional," my new friend David says. "Where did you source the roses from?"

"Well—"

"Oh no, you two can talk flowers in a second," Courtney says. "I also wanted to say that my brother is a great guy and I'm glad he met you. Our family isn't the best about sharing our feelings, but I'm going to try to get better at it."

"Thanks, Court," Connor says. His eyes look misty. "It's been an unforgettable wedding."

"I'm so fucking glad it's almost over," she says with a moan. "I'm totally never doing this again."

"I'm sure your husband will be delighted to hear that," Connor jokes.

"Anyway, have fun, you two. Dancing, dessert, drinks. Go to town."

The next hour goes by in usual wedding reception fashion, interrupted conversations, dry cake, a tad too much wine. We decide not to dance; I don't want to inflict my awkward moves on Connor in front of his entire family. Speaking of which, Connor asks me if I'll let him officially introduce me to his mom and dad as his boyfriend.

"Let's do it," I agree, fortified by the food and the wine. We find them by the cake table talking to an older couple, who drift away when we approach.

Connor's holding my hand again. It feels slightly

sweaty, but his grip is sure. "Mom, you know Shay." I nod at Iris, who smiles at me with surprising warmth. "Dad, this is Shay Brierley. My boyfriend."

"Nice to meet you, Mr. Nieves."

I let go of Connor's hand to shake his father's. "Shay. Pleased to meet you. Who does your taxes?"

"Dad." Connor sounds adorably embarrassed. "This isn't a networking event."

"Here's my card," he says, pressing an actual paper business card into my hand. "You could be missing write-offs."

"Thanks, Mr. Nieves," I say, stifling a laugh. "I'll get back to you."

"Call me Art," he says expansively. "We'll be seeing a lot of each other, I hope." He looks at Connor. "Now that Connor's decided to stay on and join the practice."

"Thanks, Art." I raise my eyebrows at Connor, who shyly smiles back. This is a new development.

"You two enjoy the party," Connor's mom says. "And Connor—we'll talk Monday, all right?"

"All right," he says.

There's a short pause, and then Connor throws his arms around his parents for a three-person hug. They pat his back awkwardly, but everyone's smiling when the embrace ends.

"By the way, it's okay if you boys want to spend time at the house. You might be more comfortable at Shay's, but you're welcome at ours," his mom adds.

Connor's cheeks color instantly. "Um. Uh. Thanks."

I just smile, since this seems like Connor's call.

Then someone says Iris's name, and the couple excuse themselves to make the rounds.

I meet Connor's gaze with mine. "That seemed to go well," I say encouragingly.

He drops his forehead to my shoulder with a groan.

"I just realized what this means. Small town. They're going to know our business. They already know I spent the night at your place like a million times."

"Six."

"Six what?"

"Six times."

"You were keeping count?"

"You weren't?"

"Okay, fine. Yes." He smiles up at me. "This grown-up relationship business is not for the faint of heart."

"Tell me about it. I should be careful what I ask for. I always wanted to be included like this, and now that I am —wow, it's intense."

He straightens up. "What—you don't like it?"

"I didn't say that. I'm just—it's an adjustment. So you're sticking around Rosedale?"

"I am," he says. "Even if my mom hadn't offered me a permanent role in the practice. Coming back here—it's been really good for me. I didn't realize how unhappy I'd been in Chicago. It's strange, I ran away to a big city where I didn't know anybody, and I thought it would let me be myself. I learned things about myself there, but in the end, I just felt...invisible. How weird is it that I had to come back to my small town in order to feel seen?"

I put my arm around his shoulders, profoundly grateful I don't have to worry about who sees me doing it.

"I'm glad you feel seen here. I don't think it's strange you had to come back to where you grew up in order to finally grow up. There's a gardening aphorism—right plant, right place. You're a Rosedale native; maybe you needed to come back to your native soil to thrive."

"What about you—you didn't grow up here."

"I'm a successful transplant," I explain. "Because I'm tenacious." I am. I may not have deep roots in Rosedale—yet. But I know I'm not going back to Scottsdale. My home is here, my future is here. Connor will be in it. Even if I don't know anything else, I know that.

EVENTUALLY, the reception starts breaking up. I've introduced Shay to what feels like every person I'm related to—and I have to give my family credit for being chill, for the most part, about my relationship status change.

But I'm exhausted from the emotional turmoil, and the long day of talking to people, and wearing uncomfortable dress shoes.

"I think we can safely take off now," I whisper to Shay, who I spot smothering a yawn. "Wanna get going?"

"Yeah. Want to come back to mine?"

I hesitate. "You sure?"

"I know your parents said we're welcome over there, but I like my own bed. Especially when you're in it."

"Then yes," I agree. "Let me say bye to Courtney."

I give my sister a fierce hug and wish her well on her Hawaiian honeymoon. Then I find Mom and tell her not to wait up, passing my keys to Dad so he can drive them home. She pats my shoulder. "Have a good night, you two."

I grab a bottle of champagne on the way out, as well as the bouquet of dahlias.

"What's that for?" Shay asks, nodding at the bottle as we make our way to the flower shop van. There's a shimmering in the air. It's snowing, not hard, just a few brave flakes.

"We have a lot to celebrate." I remind him. "This should help."

"I'm in," he says, opening the passenger door for me. "Don't mind the baby's breath. It kind of gets everywhere."

The van feels like a refrigerator after sitting all evening in the winter cold, but it still smells like petals and soil. Now everything earthy and green reminds me of Shay, and I like that. I reach for the buckle, but it's stuck on something. I tug to no avail.

"Hey, let me get that. It sticks." Shay leans across the cab with his long body, reaches across my torso, and fiddles with the belt until it comes free. He glances up at me and I smile at him, amused. He's too close not to kiss, so I do, my entire being free and light in a way I haven't felt in recent memory. His mouth gives easily under mine, and I can sense the smile on it, his thin lips curving.

We make out for a minute, the cold seeping into our bones, but I don't care. The only thing that snaps me out of the kiss is the literal snap of the buckle in the receiver at my side.

"You're all set," he says, sliding back behind the wheel.

"Thanks for the assist. Now, drive fast."

He chuckles and fires up the van. "I'm physically incapable of driving this thing fast, but I'll do my best."

He blasts the heater, which turns the cabin toasty warm in a couple of minutes.

"So, what's the deal with your parents?" I ask. "I heard they're in town."

"Oh my god, they are in town," he confirms, sounding put-upon. "They showed up unannounced—my brother, too."

"Your brother? Can I meet them?" It occurs to me that I'm such a hypocrite. "I mean, I'd like to, if you want that. I know I'm not entitled to anything—"

"Connor, stop." He glances at me, then back at the road. We're on a residential street a couple of miles from downtown. "In fact, I'll stop." He pulls the van to the side, puts it in park. "I need to say something to you, and I need you to really hear me."

"Okay."

He puts a hand on my leg. "Please stop thinking that just because we came into this from different places in our lives that we aren't on the same footing now. You told me you thought you loved me earlier tonight—that's huge. And I've never been with someone who treated me as a true partner, who honestly puts me first. I like it, being first. But don't put yourself last, okay? If you want to meet my parents, that's wonderful. I'm sure they'd love to meet you."

"But what do you want?" I ask, touched by his words, but still wanting to make sure I don't push him out of his comfort zone.

"I want you to meet them." He hesitates, then sighs. "But—"

"You don't think they'll like me?"

"What? No. You're exactly the type of guy they'd want me to end up with."

"What type of guy is that?" I smile, sensing compliments in the offing.

"You know—smart, nice, great career." He leans forward, kisses me softly. "Good with animals, fantastic kisser, knows how to find a prostate."

"Shay," I protest, laughing, if still scandalized. "Your parents don't need to know about that."

"You say that as if I haven't already told them." He smiles wickedly.

"Oh my god." I cover my face with my hands, embarrassed, even though I know he's kidding.

He pries them away gently. "All I mean is, they're going to be really happy for me. Even if it means they'll have to get on a plane to see me."

"Well, we can visit them, too, can't we? I've never been to Arizona."

"See what I mean—the perfect guy." He's smiling so hard his eyes are nearly shut, and it makes me so happy to see him this happy that suddenly my libido goes into overdrive. I need to get my hands on him. And making this van rock in the middle of the night on Wild Rose Lane seems like a bad idea.

"Let's talk more about how perfect I am when we're in your bed," I say. "Drive."

And he does.

.   .   .

A FEW MINUTES later we're in Shay's apartment, greeted by the pots of living things on every surface. As always, Shay's bedroom is warm and cozy. An oasis of tropical paradise in a frigid world. He lights the candle that makes it seem like we're making love on a grassy riverbank. We undress each other, not with the thrill of discovery but the comfort of familiarity, though the moment his nipples are revealed, I can't conceal a gasp.

"Your piercings."

He glances down. "Oh, I took them out and haven't had a chance to put them back in."

"Oh." I touch his nipples unadorned for the first time, but they feel just the same under my fingers, alive and sexy like the rest of him.

"Do you want me to put them in?"

"Whatever you want. I love them this way, too, angel."

He smiles and raises my hand from his chest to his mouth, kisses its back. "You're incredible, you know that?"

"I feel incredible when I'm with you," I answer.

After that, it's an easy, inexorable slide into each other's arms, each other's bodies. Every time we do this, it feels slightly different, each time better than the last, because we're more familiar with each other, with what makes us moan, what makes us wince, what buttons to push and which ones to avoid. Tonight, we go slow. I'm tired from the emotions of the day, but I'm not in a hurry to go to sleep. I want to wring every drop from this endless day, beyond grateful to be ending the night in bed with the man who I don't just think I love, but the man I know I'm in love with.

Shay seems just as content to tease me and bring me to the brink, then back off. He doesn't even touch my cock until I'm practically humping his thigh in desperation. Finally, he wraps his talented hand around me, and I suck in a breath. "Fuck, that feels good."

"That's what you want?" he asks, teasing me again. "You want me to stroke you off?"

"I want everything," I say, eyes rolling back in my head with how good it feels to have him touching me. "What do you want?"

"I want to ride you," he says, surprising me. "Been thinking about it since I saw your ass in those suit pants."

"But you can't see my ass when you're riding me," I respond nonsensically. "I mean, not that it matters."

"Let's just say your ass in those pants gave me lots of ideas."

"Good to know." I reach for the lube. This is still new, I'm still careful. He's strong, but he's precious. I take my time prepping him until he's shuddering beneath me. "Ready?"

"So ready, Connor."

"Come on, then." I lay back, slick up my cock before I remember I need to put on a condom. "Oh shit, I forgot—"

"It's okay. Do we really need one?"

"Um—" I blink. "No?"

"Do you want one?"

"No." That's an easier answer. "Do you?"

He bites his lip, looks almost shy. Funny, I always

think of him as in control, as the cool, calm, collected one in this relationship. "I've never done it without. But I want to with you. We can wait—"

"No." I reach up, bring him down to meet my lips. "I've wanted to since that first night. I've never done it without, either."

"Really? So I'd be your first?"

"So many of my firsts belong to you," I say. "I don't mind if you don't."

In answer, he positions himself over me, grabs my cock, and uses it to breach himself. It's immediately so tight and intense I swear loudly in the small space. It only gets more so as he drops lower. "Holy shit, you feel so fucking good," I say, resisting the urge to drive up into his body hard and fast until I release myself into him. His cheeks are red and his breathing shallow. "Are you okay?" I ask.

"Yeah, it's just—" He gets more lube onto his fingers, rises up, slicks us both up with it, then drops down again. "There's more friction this way," he says. "But it's good."

His cock bobs in front of him, long and steely hard. I wish I was flexible enough to take it in my mouth. I make do with my hand, jerking him lightly while he controls the pace of our fucking. "Doesn't feel that different," he grunts. "Maybe a little hotter?"

"It's pretty fucking hot from this spot, angel," I say. "You'll see when you do it to me."

That makes him moan and clench down on me. I buck and swear again. "Shay, I have to—"

"Yeah, do it," he says, replacing my hand on his cock with his own, while I move my hands to his hips and start pistoning up with purpose. He bounces up and down in my lap with grace that leaves me speechless except for his name.

"Shay. Yes. Fuck. Shay."

"Yeah," he urges me on, tugging at his cock. "Fill me up. You're going to leave me a mess."

"Oh god." I imagine the sticky wet evidence of our lovemaking seeping out of him and my orgasm hits me so fast and hard I can't stop it. "I'm coming, angel."

He throws his head back and speeds up the hand on his cock until I feel the splash of hot fluid on my torso, and the gush of my spend where we're joined. It's just a giant mess and I couldn't be happier about it.

"So, how did it feel?" I ask when we're mostly cleaned up and lying side by side under the covers, pretending not to care about the wet spot.

"It's a little messy, yeah," he says. "And maybe it doesn't feel that different practically. But it feels different, here—" He touches his chest over his heart. "Not to be too sappy."

"It's okay to be sappy." I kiss him and decide I better come clean about something. "Before we go to sleep, there is one more thing."

He cocks his head at me in question.

"Remember when I said I think I love you?"

"Yeah?"

"I was wrong."

His face grows still. "Oh."

"I definitely love you."

His face relaxes, his shoulders sag, and then he smiles, and he pushes on my shoulder. "Connor."

"Sorry." I laugh. "But how many times do I get to say I love you for the first time?"

"Just once," he says. "Per person, that is."

"Is it wild to think this might be the only first time for me?" I ask him, willing to bare my heart all the way. He's worth it.

He smiles softly. "Not at all."

"I love you, Shay."

"I love you, too," he whispers back. "Now go to sleep."

So we pull the quilt up and fall asleep, warm and peaceful under the covers.

SOMETHING TAPS me on the shoulder, waking me from a deep sleep.

"Angel." More tapping.

I press my face into my pillow. Maybe if I ignore it, the tapping will go away.

"Shay. We overslept. Wake up."

"Mrph?" I turn over and crack open my eyes. Connor's looking at me with anxious eyebrows. "Connor, I love you, but why am I awake right now?"

"We didn't set an alarm and the shop's supposed to be open in fifteen minutes."

I groan and turn my face to the pillow again, then sigh. "I'm opening the shop late today so I could recover from the holiday. And from you fucking my brains out last night."

"Oh shit. I didn't know," he says, sounding guilty.

I pull him down to settle on my chest, happy to be awake as long as I've got him in my arms. "It's okay. I should probably check in with my parents, anyway."

"And maybe I can meet them?" he asks hopefully.

"You can meet them," I agree, kissing the top of his head. "Pass me my phone?"

Connor reaches over me, hands me my phone from the dresser. "I just realized I don't have any clothes. Or a car. You might have to drive me home."

"What's wrong with your wedding suit? You look hot in it."

"It's sort of dressy for a Saturday morning parent meet up," he says doubtfully.

I steel myself for my two worlds to collide and sit up, knocking my head on the eve. "Dammit," I swear as I rub my head. Not an auspicious start, but then Connor kisses the sore spot, then he kisses me, and then some time passes before I remember what we're supposed to be doing.

Eventually, I tap out a text to my brother.

> Brunch? I have someone I want you guys to meet.

Tye's response comes while I'm looking for something of mine that will fit Connor.

> Mom and Dad say meet us at Hot Brew.

"I think if you wear your suit pants, you can get away with this," I say, handing him a green knit sweater that's always been small on me. "And we're on for meeting up with my family at Hot Brew."

We clean up, get dressed. When I see Connor's

cobbled-together outfit, I whistle appreciatively. "I like seeing you in my clothes, sexy."

"Yeah?" He looks down at himself self-consciously. "I look okay? I don't want to mess this up."

"They're going to love you," I promise. Maybe this get-together won't be that bad—but first, I need to fill Connor in on what happened with my family last night. "By the way, I didn't get the loan."

Connor gasps. "Oh, angel. What are you going to do?"

"I'm not sure." I haven't had time to figure out my next steps with everything else that's been going on. "But Mom and Dad wanted to set me up with my own shop. In Arizona. I told them that was not happening. In fact, yesterday I sort of yelled at them about how I'm not moving back to Scottsdale, no matter how much money they throw at me. So it might be slightly awkward, fair warning."

"Not more awkward than the circumstances under which you met my parents. I'll survive." Connor squares his shoulders, clearly up to the task. I tell myself I'll be more ready for this encounter after my flat white.

A few minutes later, we're in the reassuringly familiar environment of Hot Brew. My parents and Tye arrived first and dragged two tables together. They wave us over excitedly. I hold up a hand for them to give us a minute and order our usual from Ruth before walking over, my hand on the small of Connor's back.

I introduce everyone around, oddly nervous. "This is Connor Nieves. Connor, meet my mom, Cindy; my dad, Karl; and my brother, Tye."

My parents are on their best behavior and Connor's great with them, more relaxed than me, at least. After a few minutes of small talk, Mom asks, "Should we order food, Blueberry? Connor, what's good here?"

They walk to the counter together while Tye holds me back. "So, I take it you guys worked it out last night?"

"We did," I affirm. Tye searches my face closely. "We have more to work on. But we're both invested in this relationship. I love him." I can't help grinning when I say, "And he loves me. I know he does."

Tye presses his lips together and smiles at me. "Then I'm happy for you both, Shady," he says as we join Mom and Connor at the counter.

"Shady? Blueberry?" Connor asks.

"My family's big on nicknames," I explain. "He's Tye Dye," I say, pointing at my brother. "And he calls me Shady. For some reason, I'm Blueberry to my mom."

"It's because when you were born you had the biggest, bluest eyes, Shay," she says. "And then you loved blueberries when you were little. Of course, sometimes they made you have the most gigantic poops—"

"Okay, that's enough, Mom," I break in, mortified.

Connor laughs and I can't help an embarrassed giggle. Whatever tension there was is broken, and order food from Ruth, then settle down at the tables, chatting and laughing.

A few minutes after we start eating, I'm startled by a hand landing on my shoulder. I turn to see Jack. A part-time Rosedale resident, Kingston James, stands next to him. He's got the locs of his hair pulled back in his signature paisley print scarf. "Jack, Kingston, hey."

"Don't want to interrupt, but I had to come over and meet the family," Jack says. "Mr. and Mrs. Brierley, right? And you must be Shay's brother."

"Mom, Dad, Tye, this is Jack Avery and his friend, Kingston James."

"Jack—you're the author, aren't you?" Mom says.

"That's me. Kingston is both my friend and my book agent. Also, the reason I moved to Rosedale and met my husband, Pete."

"At your service," Kingston says, bowing in a courtly way over Mom's hand when he takes it to shake.

"Well, isn't that nice," Mom says. "Rosedale seems like a very special place."

"It really is," Jack says with feeling.

"By the way, Jack, before you hear it on the gossip circuit, I'll be joining my mom's practice permanently," Connor says.

Jack whoops. "That's awesome news. So you'll be sticking around Rosedale, then."

Connor grins at me. "I don't want to be anywhere else."

I beam back at him. "Rosedale's lucky to get another awesome veterinarian."

"So, your practice is next door to the flower shop?" my dad asks.

"That's right," Connor confirms.

"Oh, that's interesting," he says, looking at me thoughtfully.

"Jack and Kingston, won't you join us?" Mom asks.

"Oh, we can't stay," Jack says. "But it's so wonderful to meet you folks. I hope you'll visit Rosedale again soon."

"What nice men," Mom says after they leave to place an order at the counter. "And so handsome, too."

"Okay, Mom," Tye says. "Why don't you and Dad just tell Shay what you want to tell him?"

"What?" I say, my nerves returning. My parents' recent pronouncements haven't gone so well.

My dad clears his throat. "We don't have any champagne this time, but that's just as well. Shay, we thought a lot about what you said yesterday and we're sorry we were so presumptuous."

"That's right, Blueberry," Mom says sincerely. "We don't want you to live the life we want you to live—we want you to live the life you want to live. We'd just like to continue to be a part of it."

"Thanks guys," I say, blinking back unexpected tears. "That means a lot. Of course, I want you to be a part of my life."

Connor reaches under the table and entwines his hand with mine, squeezing it reassuringly.

"So we've been thinking," my dad continues, "We want to give you money for the larger down payment on the building. You should be able to qualify for a loan, no problem, and if not, we can co-sign to get you started. It's what you want, and you'll be able to keep the flower shop. Who knows, maybe this is just the beginning of your commercial real estate business."

My mouth falls open and Connor sucks in an audible breath. "Wow—I don't know what to say."

"Say yes. We gave your brother enough to buy his first franchise, and then to help with the house when he and Jen got married. We understand that franchises aren't your thing, and who knows when you'll get married —" Mom says, flicking her eyes to Connor, who tightens his grip on my hand under the table. "But you deserve this chance. And we'd be so happy to give it to you. And we promise there are no strings. Except—"

"Except?" I ask.

"Well, we were thinking maybe you, and Connor, of course, could come home for Christmas this year."

I glance at Connor, who looks delighted.

"We'd love to come for Christmas this year," I say. That part's easy. I take a deep breath. Letting them do this for me isn't the same as giving up my independence. It's letting them help me build the life I want, where I want. I look at Connor again. With the person I want. I'm beyond lucky to have parents whose love language is giving their sons large sums of money. "I accept."

"Terrific," Dad says, thumping me on the back, while Tye cheers and Mom leans over to kiss me on the cheek.

"So I just realized this means you'll not only be my mother's landlord, you'll be mine as well," Connor says.

"Yes," my dad says, brow furrowed. "Is that going to be a problem?"

I wink at my boyfriend. "I think we can make it work, right, sexy?"

"If anyone can, we can, angel," Connor says confidently. And we kiss to seal the deal, right there in Hot Brew where anyone could see.

EPILOGUE
CONNOR

Two years later

I END the call with Noelle and let out a quiet hoot. I find my mom in exam room two where she's typing some patient notes into the new computer system we implemented about six months ago. "Hey, Mom, I gotta run next door for a minute."

"Hmm?" She looks up from her notes and shoots me a quick smile. "Okay. Say hi to Shay and the girls for me."

"Will do."

I grab my coat—we're having a cold snap, but we're still waiting for that first big snow—and head out through the front office. I bend my mouth to Violet's ear. "I'll be back in five. Maybe ten."

She checks the computer. "Make it five."

"Fine." It always pays to keep on Violet's good side. Besides, it's probably better to keep it short—sometimes when I'm with Shay I lose track of time and ten minutes becomes twenty.

I jog from the practice's front door to the entrance to the flower shop and burst in. "Angel!"

My boyfriend is kneeling on the floor in front of a six-foot-tall ficus, snipping some yellowing leaves from the waxy trunk. "Hey, you," he says, glancing over his shoulder at me.

Our dogs, Ellie and Willow, middle-aged butterscotch brown mixes we acquired from one of Shay's regulars when she moved to assisted living, trot out from behind the counter and sniff me thoroughly. I give them each a kiss on the nose, then drop a kiss on Shay's mouth. Luckily he doesn't mind dog breath.

He rises elegantly and wipes his hands on his apron, then takes an elastic from his pocket and twists his hair, which flows past his shoulders at the moment, into a messy knot at the top of his head. "What's the occasion?"

"I don't have time to play coy and say I don't need a reason to visit my gorgeous boyfriend at work, though I don't."

Shay sighs. "Two years in and all the romance is gone," he says with mock plaintiveness to the dogs.

"Oh, yeah?" In three big steps, I'm at the greeting card rack. I snatch up a card I'd clocked when Shay first put it out a few weeks ago. Quickly, I grab the pen sticking out of Shay's Moleskine notebook where it sits on the counter and scribble a message over Shay's protests.

"Dude, I hope you're going to pay for that."

"Oh, I'm looking forward to paying for it," I say with a wink. I stick the card in its envelope and hand it to Shay, who takes it with a confused smile on his face.

"What's all this?"

"Open it."

He slides the card out—the cover has a line drawing of a cute boxy house complete with plants showing in every window, and a plethora of bushes and trees in the front yard. It reads "Congratulations on your new home for all your plants." He looks at me, hope and disbelief on his face. I point impatiently at the card, which he opens with shaky fingers.

He silently reads what I wrote, words that are still fresh in my mind.

Angel, the sellers accepted our offer. I can't wait to make a home with you.
All my love,
Connor

He looks at me with big watery eyes. "They did?"

I nod, blinking back my own happy tears. "We're going to be homeowners."

He laughs and sniffs and throws his arms around me. "We're getting a house."

"And a yard," I say, looking down at our dogs. "A big upgrade for you two."

For two years, we've made do with the apartment over the flower shop. We've cooked in the tiny playhouse kitchen, cohabitated with plants covering every surface, mostly successfully avoided hitting our heads on the slanted ceiling above the too-small bed. I've loved every minute of it.

I didn't officially move in until our first Christmas

together, busy as Shay and I both were. It took a while to fully integrate myself into Nieves Veterinary Care, and Shay needed to close the deal with Rodney to buy the building and make some changes at the flower shop. He hired part-time help and started offering online sales. Then he renovated the space next door to the flower shop so Charlie could set up his bike shop, which opened that June.

September found us back in Arizona for Shay's thirtieth birthday—and to meet his brand-new niece, Emilie, who had been born in July. I officially became an uncle just a few days after we got back—Courtney and Mike welcomed a girl, too, who they named Clementine. Having a baby in the family has given all of us a reason to get together more, and I've truly treasured the chance to build stronger bonds with my parents, my sister, and even Mike.

Shay and I thought about renting a bigger apartment, especially once the dogs entered our lives, but decided to stay put and save our pennies in the hopes that when we made a move, we'd be able to make it to a real house—if not our forever home, then something close to it.

Three weeks ago, Noelle at the real estate office called with what she said was "our house." It was basically a love-at-first-sight situation. The house itself is lovely, a post-war colonial that was recently updated. Four bedrooms, three baths, more than enough room for the two of us, plus Ellie and Willow. Though we're content with only fur babies at the moment, it's nice to know we have room if we want to expand our family one day.

What really sealed the deal was the solarium—an oversized sunroom attached to the south side of the house made almost entirely of glass. Shay has always wanted a greenhouse, and this is the next best thing—a place for nurturing baby plants, and where we can also put a table and chairs and soak up the sun all winter long.

When I saw his face as he visited the solarium, and then the small orchard of apple, pear, and peach trees in the large backyard, I knew I'd do anything to make this house ours.

"This is so exciting," Shay says, squeezing me tight. "I want to hear everything. What's next?"

"Noelle's got it under control. I'll fill you in later, but I have to get back before Violet comes looking for me. Mom says hi, by the way."

"Hi, Iris," Shay shouts, as if she can hear him through the wall. He and Mom get along suspiciously well now. It turns out my mom has a secret passion for bulbs, daffodils and tulips and the like, and he's been hooking her up with the biggest and best for two seasons now. "I'll let you go, but tonight we're celebrating."

"Pizza and wine?"

"Sounds perfect, sexy," he says. "Can I get a kiss before you go?"

I plant one quick kiss on his mouth. When I pull back, he's pouting. "I know, but I really have to go. Don't want to start something I can't finish."

He sighs. "You're so responsible. Fine." He lets go of me reluctantly, and if I didn't have three more patients to see before the end of the day, I'd be tempted to turn the open sign to closed and drag him behind the counter to have my way with him. "You know, this means our commutes are about to get a lot longer," he says.

I grin. It's been nice to get to work approximately one minute after I leave our place—but all things come to an end. "Worth it."

He smiles back at me. "Yeah, worth it."

Sometimes good things have to end for better things to begin.

Thank you so much for reading Shay and Connor's story! Next up, spring is on its way to Rosedale, and with it comes romance for one of my favorite characters, Kingston James, in *A Small Town Spring*.

Read on for the pecan bar recipe. (You're welcome!)

Happy reading and happy eating!

xoxo,
Elle

BECK'S PERFECT PECAN BARS RECIPE

ADAPTED FROM AMERICA'S TEST KITCHEN

For the crust:
1 cup all-purpose flour
1/3 cup brown sugar
¼ cup toasted pecans, chopped
Scant 1 teaspoon salt
¼ teaspoon baking powder
6 tablespoons unsalted butter, cut into 12 pieces and chilled

For the filling:
½ cup packed brown sugar
1/3 cup honey (can substitute maple syrup or light corn syrup)
4 tablespoons unsalted butter, melted
1 tablespoon bourbon (optional)
2 teaspoons vanilla extract
Scant ½ teaspoon salt
1 large egg, lightly beaten
2 cups toasted pecans, chopped coarse

Instructions

To toast the pecans, bake at 350 degrees F for 3-5 minutes until fragrant. Don't burn!

Heat oven to 350 degrees F. Line a 9-inch square baking pan with parchment paper or foil, and spray with nonstick baking spray.

Put the dry ingredients for the crust in a food processor and pulse a few times to combine into a dry cornmeal texture. Add the butter and pulse about ten times until you get a sandy texture. Press the mixture into the bottom of the pan and use a flat-bottomed glass or measuring cup to even the top. Bake until light brown, about 20 minutes.

While the crust is in the oven, whisk the wet ingredients for the filling together in a medium bowl.

When you remove the baked crust, pour the filling over the hot crust and sprinkle the pecans evenly on the top. Bake until cracks start to form, 22 to 25 minutes. If it doesn't crack, bake until filling seems set but still wobbly and pecans are lightly browned. Let cool to room temperature before removing from the baking pan and foil to cut using a sharp knife. Despite the size of Beck's servings, you can cut these small as they are rich. You can always have another one!

ACKNOWLEDGMENTS

It has been so much fun to play in Rosedale this year, even when the weather is chilly.

This book could not have been possible to finish without the help of my writer friends—you know who you are. In particular, I have to thank Amanda Boes and RD Black for their super detailed and thoughtful early reads, Sara Kettler for her typically incredible copy edit, Tracy at Amaze Inn Proofreading for her great work, and Dar at Wicked Smart Designs for the beautiful wintry cover.

I'm so lucky I get to do what I love on a daily basis, just like Shay and Connor. I appreciate every single person who supports me on my author journey, including every single reader. That means you!

xoxo,

Elle

ABOUT THE AUTHOR

Fueled by chocolate and canned wine, Elle Waters writes steamy, feel-good, small town romance with guaranteed happy endings. She lives with her family in Connecticut. Sign up for her newsletter at ellewatersauthor.com to hear about her next release!

Elle loves to hear from readers at elle@ellewatersauthor.com.

 facebook.com/ElleWatersAuthor

 instagram.com/ellewatersbooks

 amazon.com/~/e/B091FZQ4PZ

 bookbub.com/authors/elle-waters

www.ingramcontent.com/pod-product-compliance
Lightning Source LLC
Chambersburg PA
CBHW061122310726
48974CB00002B/639